Johnnie

Tigerskin

Books by Ursula Moray Williams

ISLAND MACKENZIE
EARL'S FALCONER
BEWARE OF THIS ANIMAL
JOHNNIE TIGERSKIN

Johnnie

❀ ❀

Tigerskin

Ursula Moray Williams

Illustrated by Diana Johns

DUELL, SLOAN AND PEARCE   NEW YORK

DUELL, SLOAN & PEARCE
AFFILIATE OF
MEREDITH PRESS

LIBRARY OF CONGRESS CATALOG CARD NUMBER: 66-13489
MANUFACTURED IN THE UNITED STATES OF AMERICA
FOR MEREDITH PRESS

TO JEHANE MARKHAM

Contents

Johnnie

❀ ❀

Tigerskin

1
Mr. Bellamy
Finds a Home

One pale, cold afternoon in early autumn a cheerful little old man with round, sparkling eyes walked down Upper Apple Street in the town of Totley, carrying a suitcase in one hand and a paper parcel in the other.

Fluffy feathers of white hair stuck out behind his ears, giving him the appearance of a happy owl. A worn brown hat sat tightly upon his bald pink head. His coat was very nice and new, but his trousers were not, and neither were his shoes, since old shoes are more comfortable to wear when one is prepared, as Mr. Bellamy was, to walk all afternoon if necessary in search of the right accommodation for himself, his suitcase, and his brown-paper parcel, which contained his tigerskin rug, called Johnnie.

Mr. Bellamy had chosen this neighborhood because he did not wish to live too far away from his great-nephews, James and Biffy Brown, and he didn't want to live too near them either. Also, he liked the name Apple Street—Upper Apple, Apple, and Lower Apple Street. It sounded friendly, homely, countrified, and domestic, as if every home stood in a little orchard and every landlady were a retired farmer's wife with an attic full of Cox's Orange Pippins.

Mr. Bellamy had lived too long in the world to be-lieve this was in the least likely to be true, but on a misty afternoon, with one end of the street blinking drowsily toward the other end, it pleased him to fancy that the lampposts were apple trees and that there was even a smell of pigs in the air.

Mr. Bellamy's niece, who was the mother of James and Biffy Brown, had told him there were rooms to let in Apple Street, and that it was a nice, clean, respect-able neighborhood to live in.

Mr. Bellamy had lately retired from being a care-taker in a big factory in the middle of England, and now with the pension that the firm had given him plus his old-age pension he felt well provided for. He was able to buy himself a new overcoat and to choose where he would like to live. He chose to live in Apple Street, near James and Biffy Brown.

So, as he trotted down the pavement with short and purposeful footsteps, his eyes darted here and there, taking in every detail of the houses that had "Rooms to Let" signs in the windows. Especially he looked to see whether the geraniums needed watering, and whether the cat sitting on the basement steps looked well fed, or was plainly used to making do with scraps from other people's garbage pails.

It was not so easy as Mr. Bellamy had expected to find a house that would suit him and Johnnie.

In Upper Apple Street the houses were bright and clean, but they had flowered carpets that the landladies would not take up, laid on the floors. Mr. Bellamy wanted a perfectly plain floor, with perhaps a linoleum, to show off the beauty of his tigerskin. In the next part of Apple Street there were plenty of linoleums, but the rooms were far too small.

At last, at the very end of Lower Apple Street, he found a cheerful little house on the corner, facing two ways. The part facing Lower Apple Street was being spring-cleaned—the other part was a post office.

It appeared to be much older than the other houses in the road, almost a left-over-from-the-country house. It was clean and newly painted. The railings had a "Wet Paint" sign dangling from them, but the painting must have been finished some time before, because a colored eiderdown was draped along the top.

A dust mop was being shaken from a window above, and as Mr. Bellamy paused outside the house, gray snowflakes of dust fell on his shoulders and settled on

his hat. Before he could brush them off, a round and shining face, tied up like a pudding in a flowered dust cap, poked out of the window, and a voice shouted, "Yes?"

"Have you got a room to let?" asked Mr. Bellamy.

"I'll come down," said the head.

Mrs. Flossey came rattling down the stairs and into Mr. Bellamy's life for ever.

2
Mr. Bellamy's New Home

The house was not spotless, but full of kindness and goodwill. Through a haze of stirred-up dust Mr. Bellamy climbed a flight of battered stairs past small, framed pictures that were constantly being rubbed askew by Mrs. Flossey's shoulders. Tower Bridge, St. Paul's Cathedral, and Marble Arch stared at him from impossible angles as he followed, yet every picture seemed to be winking with laughter. Mrs. Flossey set them rapidly to rights as she climbed, and whisked them all sideways again in turning to ask him if he minded stairs.

"A little exercise does one good," said Mr. Bellamy, arriving at the top puffing like an engine.

"I've only got the one room," Mrs. Flossey said, flinging open the door. "But it's nice."

Mr. Bellamy saw a room papered richly with roses and trellised arches. It was a new paper, and Mrs. Flossey had put it on herself. The roses did not always match—from strip to strip they clambered and chased one another, clawing at trelliswork that broke off in midair and started up underfoot as though adrift in space—but the whole effect was very cheerful. Half the ceiling had been painted white, but the floor beneath the rest of it was clean.

"That's the best part of linoleum. You can wash it," said Mrs. Flossey, scratching at some splashes with her toe. "I shall finish it tomorrow. Be ready by the afternoon. Bathroom's next door."

The bathroom was painted salmon pink, and the bathtub was just a little rusty.

"Do you like it?" said Mrs. Flossey. "There! I can see you don't!"

"I do!" said Mr. Bellamy, who had not been thinking about the bathroom at all.

"Do you mind," he said, "if I fetch my parcel from the hall?"

"I'll fetch it for you," said Mrs. Flossey. "Exercise is good for me! You sit and wait. I'll put the kettle on for tea while I'm down there."

She bounced off down the stairs like a colored beachball, and like a ball she bounced back, a few minutes later, with Mr. Bellamy's parcel in her arms.

Mr. Bellamy sat on the edge of the bathtub while

Mrs. Flossey fetched the parcel and helped him to untie the string. Then he carried it into the bedroom and spread the contents upon the un-whitewashed portion of the floor.

This was Mr. Bellamy's most treasured possession. It was Johnnie.

Flattened and creased from packing, moth-eaten in parts and worn in others, Johnnie still made Mr. Bellamy's heart beat with pride and deep affection. As he stooped to shake out the great claws, to smooth the mighty, lolling head, he forgot Mrs. Flossey gasping with admiration in the background, forgot the untidy, half-finished room, and only noticed how the light from the window lit up the tiger's stripes and reflected the gleam in his glassy but near-to-natural eyes.

The skin covered a large part of the linoleum. What matter that some of the whiskers were gone, that claws which should have been there were missing, when the rug lay there in one magnificent sweep, illumined from ivory fangs to tail tip by the last rays of winter sunshine, against a splendid background of roses and tangled trellis, a fitting frame for the King of the Jungle come to Lower Apple Street?

"It's lovely!" said Mrs. Flossey behind him, warmly, as if speaking of royalty. "I never saw anything like it in my life!"

And Mr. Bellamy knew that even if the house might never quite catch up with Mrs. Flossey's ideas, nor with anyone else's, it was the right home for himself and Johnnie, and Mrs. Flossey seemed to know it too.

"I'll make a cup of tea," she said, "and then I'll scrub that floor all over. And I'll finish the ceilings. There shan't be a speck of dirt that'll hurt it, the beautiful beast. Those roses set it off just right, don't they? You might have chosen them yourself. Now you pack it up safe, while I go down to the kettle, and by tomorrow I'll have the place right, and you can move in."

Mr. Bellamy was about to mention rental terms when a bell pealed ferociously on the lower floor.

"That'll be the post office," said Mrs. Flossey surprisingly. "Turn the kettle off, in case it's Pensions!"

She disappeared, and Mr. Bellamy followed, guided by the screaming of a kettle into Mrs. Flossey's kitchen, which was rather cold, since the windows were still wide open, and full of a variety of possessions rapidly becoming damp and chilly as darkness began to fall. Mr. Bellamy calmed the kettle and was wondering whether he ought to close the windows when Mrs. Flossey came in.

"It was Postcards, not Pensions," she explained, hurling tea leaves into the pot as if stoking the furnace of a locomotive. "D'you like it strong? I make it strong because of the geraniums." And she poured out a cup of perfectly black tea that was very welcome to Mr. Bellamy after his long pilgrimage in search of a home.

"Me front's a post office," Mrs. Flossey explained. "Opens into Dover Street. That's why I only let one room. No time for more. The bell needn't bother you much; most of the time I'm there; it's only this week I'm spring-cleaning in between. I can bring your meals upstairs or you can have them with me, just as you like.''

Mr. Bellamy, thinking of the open windows, said he would have his meals upstairs until the spring-cleaning was over, and Mrs. Flossey nodded as if this were a very wise suggestion.

After tea he left his tigerskin in Mrs. Flossey's charge without a qualm and trotted down two streets and up a third till he came to the house of his niece, Mrs. Brown. Rather to his relief, he found her alone.

''James and Biffy are out with their friend Sarah. They will be coming to see you soon,'' said Mrs. Brown, pouring out a cup of very pale-colored tea for him.

''I have had tea, thank you,'' said Mr. Bellamy.

''I won't pour it away. It will be good for the ferns,'' said Mrs. Brown. ''I'm glad you are suited, Uncle. Is it a nice clean kind of place?''

''Well, not yet,'' said Mr. Bellamy truthfully. ''But it is going to be.''

''H'm,'' said Mrs. Brown. ''Good furniture? Good style? Good bed?''

''I didn't try it,'' confessed Mr. Bellamy.

''Didn't try the *bed?* What's the food like?'' asked Mrs. Brown.

''I only had a cup of tea,'' confessed Mr. Bellamy.

''Funny you choosing a place like that,'' said Mrs. Brown. ''If only you'd have mentioned it I'd have come with you. Well, you must stay here for the night until she's got it ready for you. Got your luggage?''

"I only have a suitcase," said Mr. Bellamy. "I left my tiger with Mrs. Flossey."

"You did that?" said Mrs. Brown, opening her eyes very wide. "You've changed a lot, Uncle Bellamy, to leave that rug of yours with strangers."

But already Mr. Bellamy felt that Mrs. Flossey was a friend and not a stranger.

That night when he lay in Biffy's bed with a spiky pair of Dinky toys jabbing at his feet he could still see her dusty shining face and the admiration in her eyes as she gazed at Johnnie.

Dearly as he loved his niece, Mrs. Brown, and his great-nephews, James and Biffy, he could hardly wait to go back to Lower Apple Street and begin life in his new home.

"You come back here if she doesn't feed you properly," Mrs. Brown said, as she saw him off after dinner next day. "There are plenty of nice houses up that road. I don't see why you had to go and pick on the Post Office. I should have thought she'd have enough to do without you to look after."

But Mrs. Flossey welcomed Mr. Bellamy back like a relation.

"Your room's ready," she told him. "And the kettle's on for tea when you're done."

A bedspread of the same color as the roses was on the bed, a black satin cushion on the chair.

Johnnie lay at ease in a kingdom of ornaments, colored china plates, pot plants, and tradesmen's calendars, on a newly scrubbed linoleum reflecting a ceiling that was drying almost faster than it was advertised to do.

A gas fire roared hotly over the scene, while in the bathroom new towels flanked the salmon-colored tub like slices of cool green cucumber.

Mr. Bellamy glowed with pleasure.

"I'll bring up your tea!" said Mrs. Flossey. "And then I'll get on with my work, if you don't mind. I'm doing out the post office now with bluebell wallpaper, and some of the silly stuff is printed upside down."

3

Sarah

The cup of tea, Mrs. Flossey's kindness, and his own contentment lulled Mr. Bellamy to sleep. After his second cup he sat back in his chair in front of the gas fire and dozed off.

He was awakened by Mrs. Flossey's brisk rap at the door.

"Two young men to see you!" she cried, at the same time opening the door and ushering in James and Biffy, who had chosen to pass by Lower Apple Street on their way home from school.

Mr. Bellamy was glad he had not yet eaten Mrs. Flossey's jam tarts from the shop which was part of the Post Office. Great-nephews, he knew, were always very hungry. When he got settled down he meant to keep a large supply of cookies and cakes and good things so that James and Biffy would always get a welcome when they arrived. And just sometimes, he reflected, he would be out at teatime.

James and Biffy ate the tarts, their eyes absorbing and admiring every detail of the room, but coming back over and over again to rest on the tigerskin which was the center of it all. It stood out like some glorious work of art against the background of a minor exhibition.

"Did you shoot it, Uncle Bellamy?"

"No, James and Biffy, I have told you many times I did not."

"Did you buy it alive then?"

"No."

"Did you ever shoot a tiger, Uncle Bellamy?"

"No, I am afraid I did not."

"Why?"

Mr. Bellamy replied stiffly, "Because I have never been to India."

"Who did shoot it then?" asked James and Biffy.

"My brother Humber."

"Was he an Indian?"

"No. He was an Englishman who traveled in India."

Mr. Bellamy knew that if their mother had been there James and Biffy would not have dared to ask so many questions, and he was about to say so when Mrs. Flossey came bounding up the stairs with another plate of cakes and jam tarts.

"And now we had better be going," said James when

the cakes were finished. "We promised we would go straight home after school."

"Coming to have tea with me is hardly going straight home after school," said Mr. Bellamy reprovingly.

"They came to see how their uncle was getting on," Mrs. Flossey excused them. "They're lovely boys!"

James and Biffy lay flat on the floor before they left, to stroke the top of the tiger's head. "Next time we come," said James, "we will bring our friend Sarah with us. She is simply longing to see Johnnie."

Mr. Bellamy invited them to bring their friend Sarah to tea on Sunday.

"They're lovely boys!" Mrs. Flossey repeated, sweeping up the crumbs when James and Biffy were gone. "Well, I'd better be going now. Shall I fill up the pot again?"

On Saturday afternoon, Mr. Bellamy bought crumpets and cream slices and éclairs and chocolate cookies for this tea party on Sunday. While he was out, Mrs. Flossey polished the floor and brushed the tigerskin so vigorously that some of the hairs came out. She was very upset, and apologized to Mr. Bellamy.

"I didn't know it would spoil like that," she said regretfully. "Looks as if the moths had got at it before I did!"

Since her intentions had been so excellent, Mr. Bellamy forgave her at once. What was left of the rug looked much improved by the brushing. The black stripes fairly shone.

Mrs. Flossey went down to fetch her best china for the tea party, anxious to make up for her carelessness by doing all she could to help and to please. The table looked very attractive with the cakes, the pretty china, and the colored paper napkins. Mrs. Flossey said the boys could toast the crumpets at the gas fire when they came.

"It will make a change for them having a little girl to play with," she said. "It's nice for boys to have little girls to tea now and then. Makes a change for them, like."

What neither Mrs. Flossey nor Mr. Bellamy knew was that, far from being a change, James and Biffy were never without their friend Sarah for a single moment if they could avoid it. They called for her on their way to school and took her home afterward. First thing on Saturday morning they were waiting at her gate. On Sundays they spent most of the day together.

It was Sarah who had sent James and Biffy on their first visit to Mr. Bellamy—waiting for them outside Mrs. Flossey's house, where she hopped up and down on the railings, and pretended to be waiting for some-one quite different.

"Well?" she said on their return. "Didn't your Uncle Bellamy ask to see me?"

"He asked us to bring you to tea on Sunday," said James and Biffy, and Sarah was quite satisfied. "I shall look forward to that," she said.

If Mrs. Flossey and Mr. Bellamy expected Sarah to be a typical pretty little girl with curly hair, they were quite mistaken. Sarah was tall and thin, with long, jumpy legs that she liked to cover with jeans rather than with skirts and dresses. Her face was pale and pointed. She turned her head and looked straight at people out of eyes that nearly everyone thought were black, but they were really dark blue. Her eyebrows were like thin birch twigs across her forehead, turning up a little at the edges. She had a shower of small freckles on the bridge of her nose. Sarah's eyesight was excellent, but for some reason best known to her-self she liked to carry a pair of spectacles in her pocket, which she put on in company. James and Biffy loved her dearly, but their mother did not care for her very much. For one thing, Sarah said such odd things.

"My great-great-grandmother was a witch!" said Sarah. "She was burned at the stake!"

"Sarah!" said Mrs. Brown.

"We still have the stake," Sarah said, staring straight into Mrs. Brown's eyes. "It is used in our family as a walking stick."

Afterward their mother told James and Biffy that Sarah just made up things, they were not really true.

"But we want them to be true!" said James and Biffy.

They brought Sarah to Mrs. Flossey's house in Lower Apple Street at four o'clock on Sunday afternoon. She wore a little round black hat of her mother's and jeans. Her hair was tied in two little black pigtails, one on either side of her face.

Mrs. Flossey thought she looked peculiar, but James and Biffy were very proud to be introducing her to their Uncle Bellamy, and very impressed by her good manners as she walked across the room to shake his hand, not even glancing at the tigerskin about which she had heard so much.

"How do you do, my dear," said Mr. Bellamy kindly. "How do you do, Sarah."

"That is the tiger," said Biffy. "He's called Johnnie."

Sarah put on her glasses, and dropping to the floor kissed the tigerskin reverently on the nose. "It is so beautiful!" she murmured.

But after tea she began to find fault. "Why has it three claws on one paw and four on another? Why are there bald patches on its ears? On its flanks? On its tail? Where have its whiskers gone?"

To all Mr. Bellamy's explanations she answered, "Oh!" He found himself apologizing for his tiger.

"It is more than fifty years old," he explained to her. "It was shot by my brother Humber, quite early in the century."

"Our Great-uncle Humber," James added impressively.

"Poor, poor creature!" she said, stroking the tiger as if to comfort it for Uncle Humber's cruelty. She ran her fingers over Johnnie's flanks.

"Where is the bullet hole?" she asked. "There must be a bullet hole. When the sheriff in Texas shot my grandfather, there was a round bullet hole right through the calf of his leg. Quite round. Right through the calf."

"Is that true?" asked Mr. Bellamy.

"It must be true," said James and Biffy. "Sarah always tells it to us."

They searched the fur for a bullet hole.

"I only see moth holes," said Sarah.

Mr. Bellamy was distressed. His one passion had been to keep Johnnie free from damage by moths and other insects. It was as if Sarah had hit him.

"My mother has some very good moth powder," said Sarah, comforting him. "It is used by the Queen."

"Does the Queen get *moth?*" said Biffy in astonishment.

"It is used by the Queen in her *tigerskins,*" said Sarah severely.

"That's an old-fashioned one, that is," said Mrs.

Flossey when Sarah was gone. "But those boys—
they're lovely!"

Some time after school had finished the next evening
Sarah was back with a can of moth-destroying powder,
and James and Biffy in close attendance. They dusted
the rug all over till the tiger was gray, and the bald
patches stood out like pools of stagnant water on a
rugged heath.

"The moths will be dead in the morning," said
Sarah.

Mr. Bellamy sneezed all night because of the powder,
and he did not find any dead moths in the morning, but
he thought it was kind of Sarah to take the trouble.
Most children would have forgotten all about it.

In the days that followed he saw quite a lot of her.
He soon began to realize that whenever he saw James
and Biffy he would see Sarah too. He saw rather too
much of her really. And yet one could not help getting
a little bit fond of Sarah.

She was always polite. She never shook hands with
him without making a little bob, as if at dancing class,
when saying how-do-you-do and good-bye. She did the
same with Mrs. Flossey, only the fraction of a millionth
less politely.

"You are a well-brought-up little girl," Mr. Bellamy
told her one day. James and Biffy beamed as if the
compliment had been for them.

"Yes," said Sarah, and sighed.

"You may tell your parents I said so," said Mr.
Bellamy kindly.

"Thank you," said Sarah. "I have no father, and actually I don't expect my mother will be interested; she is always out at parties and I hardly ever see her at all."

"Well, that explains a lot," Mrs. Flossey said when Mr. Bellamy repeated this remark to her. "I always thought there was something odd about that one."

Mrs. Flossey did not like Sarah as much as Mr. Bellamy did. But then Sarah had won her way into Mr. Bellamy's heart through her love of Johnnie. In spite of her early criticisms she worshiped Johnnie. Sometimes it seemed there had never been a time when Sarah had not been seated on the floor with Johnnie's head in her lap, fondling his ears or running her fingers over his worn patches. (Mr. Bellamy wished she would not do that.)

"It seems so sad he is dead," said Sarah. "I would like to bring him to life again."

"If Johnnie were alive he would be roaming the jungle," said Mr. Bellamy. "There would hardly be room for him in Lower Apple Street, Totley."

"He might be in the zoo," said James.

"Or the circus," said Biffy.

"I am sure he is much happier lying on the floor with his head on Sarah's knee," said Mr. Bellamy.

"I brought our parrakeet to life," Sarah said, fixing her eyes on Mr. Bellamy. "The cat had it and left it lying upside down on the floor. It was stone dead. I picked it up and gave it the kiss of life, and it lived again. It was a miracle."

"It can't have been quite dead," said Mr. Bellamy.

"It *was,* Uncle Bellamy. Sarah has told us lots of times!" said James and Biffy.

"I did it to a stuffed alligator too," Sarah said. "It was in somebody's collection."

Mr. Bellamy did not think Sarah always told the truth.

One day when she had actually gone to the dentist by herself he said so to the boys.

"I don't think you should believe all that Sarah says," he began. "I'm afraid she doesn't always tell the truth."

"We know she doesn't," his great-nephews agreed promptly. "But we believe her. She's so *interesting!*"

"I hope *you* always tell the truth," said Mr. Bellamy severely.

"Yes, we do," said James. "We have to, because of Daddy and Mummy. And we don't know how to make up beautiful lies like Sarah does."

"I am very glad to hear it," said Mr. Bellamy, greatly relieved.

The next day he told Sarah that neither he nor Mrs. Flossey liked the stories she told that were not true.

Mrs. Flossey had just relented for a moment toward Sarah, and allowed her to come and serve in the part of the post office that sold a few groceries and packets of chocolate. "It isn't her fault," she reproached Mr. Bellamy. "She hasn't got a good mom and dad like those boys have. You can't expect it of her."

Sarah looked at them both with her straight stare.

"Actually I am going to a doctor about it," she said solemnly. "I don't like telling lies any more than you do. I've got an appointment with him this evening. Golly!" she exclaimed, looking at the tiny watch on her skinny wrist. "I'm late! James! Biffy! Come on! You've got to take me up to Rafford Street." They were all in the little post office where Mrs. Flossey was just packing up for the night. As Sarah and the boys made a dive for the door, it opened with a clang of the bell, and they cannoned into a well-dressed stranger.

The stranger seized Sarah by the arm, and she exclaimed, "Daddy!"

"So here you are, my girl!" said the stranger in a cheerful voice. "Mrs. Brown told me where you were likely to be. Now, look, I've got a message from Mommy. It's the fifth night you've been out after six. If you aren't in the house by a quarter past sharp, she won't read you *The Wind in the Willows,* and if you're two minutes after that, I shan't come and kiss you good night."

"What d'you make of that!" gasped Mrs. Flossey.

"I'm sorry about this," said Sarah's father, grinning. "She's supposed to come straight home after school, but we thought she was at the Browns'."

"Daddy, you must see Johnnie! Uncle Bellamy, can he? Do let him see Johnnie!" cried Sarah, not in the least abashed, and hopping about between her father and Mr. Bellamy.

She was so persistent that Mr. Bellamy found himself leading the way upstairs with Sarah's father behind him and James and Biffy in the rear.

"You said he was *dead!*" they whispered to Sarah angrily.

"Ssh! He's secret service. Everybody thinks he's dead!" she murmured. "He rescues people from behind the Iron Curtain. He's just on leave!" she added persuasively. James and Biffy could not compete with Sarah, who now displayed the tigerskin to her father as if Johnnie were her very own.

Mr. Bellamy was anxious to get his room to himself so that he could sit down and think things out.

"I think Sarah said she had an appointment," he hinted to her father. "With a doctor, wasn't it—a psychiatrist or something?"

"Sarah can have an appointment with anyone who will tan her bottom for her!" said her father cheerfully. "But I think her only date is Home to Bed."

They watched her dancing up Apple Street, hanging onto her father's arm. Halfway up she pulled a handkerchief out of his pocket and waved it, twisting and hopping backward till both of them were out of sight.

4

No More Sarah

That finished Sarah, for the time being. Both Mr. Bel-
lamy and Mrs. Flossey said she was not to come to the
house unless she was specially invited. Mrs. Brown,
when appealed to, said she quite agreed.

Biffy and James were upset. They loved their Great-
uncle Bellamy, and they loved Sarah. And most of all,
perhaps, they loved Johnnie. They might have per-
suaded Mr. Bellamy to change his mind, but Mrs. Flossey was adamant. She locked the Lower Apple Street
door so that everyone had to come in through the post
office. When James and Biffy came in from school with
Sarah close on their heels she greeted them with,
"Come in, you-and-you. Now, Sarah, have you been
invited?"

Sarah tried every excuse in turn: "I came with James and Biffy," "I only meant to stop a minute," "I just wanted to see Johnnie," or "I just wanted to see Mr. Bellamy."

"Mr. Bellamy will tell me when he wants to see you!" snapped Mrs. Flossey, closing the door on her.

"I'll wait outside. You ask him," Sarah urged James and Biffy. But she soon grew tired of waiting and went away, while all Mr. Bellamy would say was, "Well, I think it is really just as well," when they told him how unkind Mrs. Flossey had been to Sarah.

"Why don't you like her?" said James and Biffy.

"I do like her, but I don't like her complete disregard for the truth," said Mr. Bellamy firmly. "I was brought up to have a horror of lies."

"Uncle Bellamy doesn't like your lies," James told Sarah on their way to school.

"They don't do any harm," said Sarah sadly. "They do good. When we made paper darts in class, I said I'd made them all, every one. Miss Bartley couldn't think how one little girl could make so many in just a few minutes, and she sent me in to Miss Anderson. Miss Anderson couldn't think either, but I told her how my father was a leading aircraft engineer, and how he'd developed everything from paper darts, and so of course I had it in the blood. None of the rest of the class got punished, only me."

"Then *they* were telling lies," said Biffy.

"No, they weren't. Nobody asked them," said Sarah.

"I bore the whole burden myself. You should tell your Uncle Bellamy that."

"He'd think it silly, and so do I," said James. "If you hadn't said that, there would only have been about thirty *little* punishments instead of one big one."

"What I really mind about is Johnnie!" sighed Sarah, changing the subject. "I long to see Johnnie! I miss him so. Do tell Uncle Bellamy how badly I miss him—Johnnie, I mean, not Uncle Bellamy."

But Uncle Bellamy only shook his head and smiled, and although Sarah bought stamps at the post office on two days running and a postal order on the third, she never caught a glimpse of Johnnie, and Mrs. Flossey served her so quickly that she had no hope of creeping out behind the shop, or even of opening the door and peeping up the stairs.

She wrote a letter to Johnnie and posted it, with a stamp in case James and Biffy should forget to deliver it, or in case it should fall into the hands of Mrs. Flossey.

"She would be sure to destroy it if it did," Sarah said darkly, explaining to the boys about the letter.

"She wouldn't—she's much too kind," said James and Biffy.

"Not to *me*," said Sarah forlornly.

Mr. Bellamy showed them the letter when it arrived.

DEAR, DEAR JOHNNIE,

I miss you so much and all night long I dream about tigers. Do ask Uncle Bellamy if I can come and see you again. Please do tell him I miss him too, very terribly. I miss you both so much, I cry and cry.

Your loving Sarah

"I do think she is very sad about it," James agreed, handing the letter back.

"It is breaking her heart!" said Biffy.

"She's a clever one," said Mrs. Flossey, bringing in the tea. "Break her heart! Not that one! Don't you believe her!"

But Mr. Bellamy could not bear even to run the risk of breaking Sarah's heart, and he invited Sarah to come to tea again, and lectured her very seriously about telling the truth.

Sarah sat on the floor nursing Johnnie's head, and looking at Mr. Bellamy with her large, round eyes.

"This is the happiest day of my life!" she said, stroking the tiger's jet-black stripes. "This is the day when I came back into your house, and the day when I decided to tell the truth always, for ever after. It is almost better than Christmas Day."

"Father Christmas doesn't bring much to fibbers," said Mrs. Flossey, clearing away. "He'll be writing up his lists right now, Sarah, and yours won't take him long."

"On the contrary, I am going to have a tape recorder," returned Sarah.

"Now then! Now then!" reprimanded Mrs. Flossey.

"She isn't!" said James and Biffy.

"Now, careful, Sarah!" admonished Mr. Bellamy.

"I *am* going to have a tape recorder for Christmas,"

said Sarah with a contemptuous sniff. Nobody said anything, but a feeling of embarrassment affected everybody except Sarah, who jumped to her feet, took the tray from Mrs. Flossey, and carried it down below. She could soon be heard washing up the tea things, and singing carols at the top of her voice.

Mr. Bellamy and Mrs. Flossey shook their heads, and smiled ruefully at each other. Sarah was not a problem that could be solved in one afternoon.

Christmas came nearer, day by day.

To Mr. Bellamy it was just a procession of rather sunless afternoons, on some of which his great-nephews came and on some of which they did not. There were several Sundays, on each of which he went to church in the morning and to tea at James and Biffy's house in the afternoon. One Wednesday there was a carol concert at James and Biffy's school, and he went to listen to it with Mrs. Brown. He forgot that Sarah attended the same school as they did. She stood up alone and sang a verse of "The Holly and the Ivy" all by herself, while James and Biffy were merely in a junior chorus singing "The First Noël," and one could not distinguish their voices at all.

"Excellent! Excellent!" said Mr. Bellamy, turning to Mrs. Brown. But Mrs. Brown was not applauding.

"Sarah likes to show off," she said. "I am thankful that we shall have a vacation from her at Christmas."

Mrs. Flossey had invited her sister to spend Christmas at the post office, while Mr. Bellamy had been asked to pass three days with James and Biffy and

their parents. After some deliberation he decided not
to take Johnnie with him. Johnnie would be quite safe
in Mrs. Flossey's care, and might have rather an exact-
ing time with James and Biffy rampaging all over
the house during the holiday. Already, Mr. Bellamy
thought, Johnnie looked a little the worse for wear
since he came to Lower Apple Street—partly due to
Mrs. Flossey's brushings, partly to Sarah's strokings,
and partly to the lively feet of James and Biffy.

"That's all right," said Mrs. Flossey. "Nobody will
hurt it up there. I'll turn the key in the door, and everything will be just as it was till you come back."

"Of course, if the boys are very disappointed I could
always fetch it," said Mr. Bellamy.

"That's right. It isn't far to come," agreed Mrs.
Flossey. "Don't you worry about a thing."

Sarah invented no more fantastic tales about her
forthcoming Christmas. She seemed to be trying sin-
cerely to tell the truth.

"Ask no questions and you will be told no lies!" she
had a habit of repeating when James and Biffy became
inquisitive. It seemed as if her Christmas Day would be
the same as many other children's—church in the
morning, walk in the afternoon, and a big meal with
turkey in the evening. She even had some cousins coming to stay, but Sarah did not seem very interested in
them. She brought a Christmas card for Mrs. Flossey
to Lower Apple Street, on the day before Christmas
Eve, and a paper decoration to put round Johnnie's

neck. Then she said "Happy Christmas!" to everyone, and just disappeared.

"It seems funny to think we shan't see Sarah again for three whole days," said James sadly.

Somehow it took a little of the fun away from Christmas.

5

Christmas Eve

Mr. Bellamy arrived to spend Christmas at his niece's home, and found a great welcome awaiting him. The boys had decorated the house from top to bottom in his honor. Paper garlands crossed the room in large festoons, so that grown-ups had to proceed at a kind of crouch, or be tickled by dangling tails of silver foil that twirled solemnly in the heat.

A spread of colored paper bearing a Christmas scene stretched from one end of the mantelpiece to the other, while paper lanterns hung from picture rails and door handles, and dimmed the light of the central electric bulb. Christmas cards swooped on strings from all corners of the room, and James had ingeniously covered

the television screen with transparent red paper,
through which a Western glowed without very much
meaning, but it added an air of mystery to the gaiety
of the room.

Upstairs, Mr. Bellamy found his bedroom bright
with streamers, tinsel, and evergreens. The boys had
made a snow scene on his bedside table, complete with
little plaster houses and polar bears. An electric stove
was burning, and it was very cosy and cheerful.

"We left room for Johnnie *downstairs,*" said James
and Biffy pointedly.

"I didn't bring Johnnie with me," Mr. Bellamy confessed.

James and Biffy looked at him reproachfully.

"Oh, what a pity!" they said. Mr. Bellamy felt he
had not played his part. They had done so much to
make him welcome, and now he had let them down. He
did not know what to say.

"It doesn't matter," said James politely. "Come
downstairs and have tea."

They had a Christmas Eve tea, with Mr. Brown
cracking jokes and everyone delighted to see Uncle
Bellamy.

Afterward James and Biffy took away the tea things
and, without being asked, washed them to help their
mother.

"Bless them, they've been ever so helpful lately,"
said Mrs. Brown. "They're much better without that
Sarah."

When the dishes were done they all sat around the

fire and watched television, after James had taken away the red paper, which was pretty but spoiled the picture. The program was all about wild life in the jungle, and it made Mr. Bellamy feel guilty again, as if he had let down Johnnie as well as his great-nephews. He determined to go and fetch the tigerskin in the morning. It would make Christmas complete.

Halfway through the program they all became aware of an outside noise—faint, because of the door and the sound of the television, but persistent, as if it intended to be heard, and it was not very far away.

"Carol singers!" said Mrs. Brown in annoyance. "We've had them nearly every night since November. Don't take any notice of them!"

But in the picture the jungle had become suddenly very quiet, and the carolers sang louder and louder.

"Good, aren't they?" said Mr. Brown, who enjoyed music. "Better than what we had last night. Maybe it's the Chapel."

Mrs. Brown jumped up abruptly and switched off the television.

"Oh, no! Oh, Mom!" exclaimed James and Biffy.

"Listen!" said Mrs. Brown.

Only a large and well-trained choir could be singing "Silent Night" as well as the singers outside the closed window. Mrs. Brown peeped through the curtains. "Can't see a thing!" she declared. "They haven't got a light between them. It must be the Chapel. Where's my purse? Got any silver on you, Dad?"

Grudgingly Mr. Brown handed over two sixpences.

"Don't throw it at them. Let them go on a bit. I'm enjoying it," he said. "They're good. They're every bit as good as St. Luke's Church choir down the road."

Mr. Bellamy found half a crown. "I don't hear them much up in my flat, and Mrs. Flossey doesn't encourage them," he explained. "They certainly sing well. Makes me think of my young days, when we all sang in the choir. We thought the world of our Christmas services."

"Can I turn the television on again?" said Biffy plaintively. He and James were not allowed to go out carol-singing, so they had no interest in those who did.

"Just wait till it's finished. There, that's lovely!" said Mrs. Brown as the carol came to a harmonious close. "Go and open the door, Biff, and give them this."

"We'll all go," said Mr. Brown, rising to his feet. Mr. Bellamy got up too, feeling quite young again at the thought of meeting a real choir of carol singers.

They all trooped to the front door and opened it wide. Mr. Brown switched on the porch light.

On the doorstep, wearing her glasses and her mother's little round black hat, was Sarah, all alone, except that she had Johnnie draped the whole way around her shoulders, and at her feet was an open tape recorder.

Doors were opening to left and right, and even opposite, as neighbors came out to see who the magnificent choir could be. It seemed better to pull Sarah indoors and shut the door before asking for an explanation. James and Biffy carried in the tape recorder.

"I hope you enjoyed it," Sarah said. "I took it in the porch at St. Luke's Church this afternoon. Nobody noticed. And then I went and fetched Johnnie. Johnnie is very fond of carols."

"But how did you get Johnnie?" said Mr. Bellamy, lifting the tigerskin from Sarah's shoulders. "And who told you you might go and take him from my room?"

"Mrs. Flossey did, when I took her Christmas present," said Sarah blandly. "I said you wanted him after all. Didn't you want him after all?" she added sweetly.

"I did, but—I can't understand Mrs. Flossey allowing it," said Mr. Bellamy, nonplussed.

"Actually she thought I was fetching your raincoat," Sarah admitted without a blush. "You see, I never tell lies nowadays, so I did fetch your raincoat too. I put Johnnie on first and your raincoat on top. It's hanging on the gate now, Biffy. I had a lovely, lovely time with Mrs. Flossey. I played her St. Luke's carols on my tape recorder, and what they said at the fish-and-chip shop where I went down to last night. Nobody noticed. Mrs. Flossey laughed and laughed, and so did her sister. We all had sherry and port!"

"Sarah!" said Mrs. Brown.

"Well, not me," said Sarah hastily. "But I poured out for the others. Just for Christmas, Mrs. Flossey said. And then I fetched Johnnie and came on here."

By now Sarah was sitting on top of Johnnie in the middle of the floor in front of the fire, and they were all sitting around her.

"So you did get a tape recorder," said James.

Sarah nodded. "It is really my Christmas present, but they gave it to me early to keep me quiet," she explained. "I got so excited about my cousins' coming."

"And now your cousins have come, you are out!" said Mrs. Brown severely.

"Oh, well! They'll be here for days, and Christmas has only just begun," said Sarah. "Your decorations are very beautiful. Haven't you got a Christmas tree? Ours is all silver ..."

At that moment there came an agitated ringing at the bell. Mrs. Flossey was on the doorstep, quite upset. She seemed greatly relieved to see Sarah sitting on the tigerskin.

"I thought I was doing right, Mr. Bellamy, but afterward it came over me I ought to have gone up and fetched your raincoat myself," she said. "And when I saw the tigerskin had gone off the floor I nearly dropped down dead. She never said a word about fetching the rug. You're a sly one, that's what you are, young Sarah, not to tell me what you were after when you went up those stairs."

Sarah dropped her eyes and looked at the floor.

"It was kind of Sarah to think I might be wanting Johnnie and my extra raincoat," said Mr. Bellamy, who did not want to spoil the happy atmosphere of Christmas Eve. "I am sure she will apologize for worrying you, and for bringing you out at this time of night. It was very kind of you to come."

"I am extremely sorry for worrying you," said Sarah to Mrs. Flossey, "but as it is over and done with now, I do think it is very nice to have you with us in this beautiful room on Christmas Eve. We are all of us together now, with Johnnie. It is quite perfect."

To calm everybody down Mrs. Brown made cocoa and handed around a bottle of ginger cordial. Sarah handed out presents she had brought for James and Biffy and Mr. Bellamy. James and Biffy each had a rubber dagger which looked very fierce, while Mr. Bellamy had a can covered with Christmas paper and full of pills.

"There are all kinds there," Sarah explained, "so whatever illness you have got, you will have a cure."

Mr. and Mrs. Brown and Mr. Bellamy almost bounced out of their chairs.

"It was a kind thought, Sarah, but you should never, *never* play with pills. You might kill somebody," said Mr. Bellamy.

"I know, my auntie did once," said Sarah calmly, adding hastily, "I mean she might have if she had."

"Had what?" asked James and Biffy.

"Nothing," said Sarah. "I mean, that is why the pills are all made of cardboard!" Mr. Bellamy looked again and saw that they were. He felt like shaking Sarah.

"Did your auntie really, Sarah?" asked Biffy.

"No, she didn't, as a matter of fact," said Sarah with complete frankness. "She had a little box just like this, and she used it for collar studs. Shall I put on the fish-shop tape?''

As nobody said ''No, don't,'' Sarah did, and for a long time nobody laughed, but when they began they could not stop laughing. Sarah packed up her tape recorder and left quietly for home. Mrs. Flossey left too.

On the whole it was a very happy Christmas.

6

Johnnie at the Zoo

Suddenly there was no more Sarah. She just stopped going about with James and Biffy. All through the Christmas holidays she came only twice to Mr. Bellamy's flat, and then she was totally absorbed with her tape recorder and nearly deafened them all with a rendering of church bells clanging very much too loudly.

"I am extremely busy," she told the boys. "I record everything—the trains, the traffic, people talking, children crying, boys shouting. I have got a hen laying an egg. I switched it on when my mother had people to tea, and it surprised everybody very much. They were down on their hands and knees looking under the sofa while my mother fetched the scones. Then I just walked

in and switched it off, behind the sofa. My mother
went quite pink with rage, but the people laughed.''

''You should be ashamed of yourself,'' said Mr. Bellamy.

''Were you punished?'' asked James and Biffy.

''No, of course not!'' said Sarah, tossing her head.
''That's nothing to what I mean to do with it.''

''One day you'll go too far,'' warned Mr. Bellamy.

Sarah just laughed and carried her machine away.
She seemed to be always walking sideways somewhere
and hugging it these days. James and Biffy would have
dearly loved to go with her, but Sarah did not want
them. Sometimes they saw her climbing into buses on
some mysterious expedition, always with the tape recorder beside her. She waved to them in an absent kind
of way, but it was quite clear that she did not need
their company. James and Biffy were hurt, and the
holidays dragged out, with long, cold days and long,
cold gaps between mealtimes. To comfort them, Mr.
Bellamy invited them to go to the London Zoo. He had
not been there himself for many years, and it gave him
quite a thrill to go again with his great-nephews.

They came to lunch at Mrs. Flossey's first, rather
early so as to catch the Green Line bus outside the
post office. Mrs. Flossey had been invited to go too,
but she could not leave the post office to look after
itself and was obliged to say no. But she cooked them
an excellent dinner, which they ate sitting around the
table in her little room, with one eye on the clock in
case they missed the bus.

"We have ten minutes before the bus comes," said Mr. Bellamy when dinner was over. "You had better go upstairs and wash your hands, and then we will wait outside on the corner."

James and Biffy went upstairs, but before they had had time to wash, both came pelting down as though from catapults.

"Uncle Bellamy! Can we take Johnnie? Oh, *please,* can we take Johnnie to the zoo?"

"Take Johnnie?" said Mr. Bellamy in amazement.

"Oh, yes, Uncle Bellamy! Do let's take Johnnie to see the real tigers and lions! He's far, far more handsome than they are, and he'll like to see them so much!"

"But how can we take him?" said Mr. Bellamy, rather dazed.

"In a parcel, Uncle Bellamy, all wrapped up!" said James and Biffy. "We can unwrap him when we look at the tigers and wrap him up again after. Don't you want to see him next to the real ones, Uncle Bellamy?" they said.

Mr. Bellamy did. He was just as sure as James and Biffy that Johnnie was the biggest and most beautiful tiger that had ever come out of India, and the idea of making a comparison appealed to him very much indeed.

"Very well, we will take Johnnie to the zoo," he agreed.

The boys went wild with joy, but there was little time for celebrating, since time was running out; Johnnie had to be folded and wrapped up, and tied in a stout

brown-paper parcel suitable for carrying on the bus.
Then they all called good-bye to Mrs. Flossey, who was
so busy serving a customer with National Insurance
stamps that she did not even look up and ask what
on earth they were carrying, as she certainly would
have done had she been free to notice the parcel.

The Green Line bus was punctual, and there were
seats for all three, with Johnnie on Mr. Bellamy's lap.
He allowed James to pay for the fares, out of a ten-
shilling note. They set off for the London Zoo.

More than one curious eye was cast over the large
parcel that Johnnie made when they arrived at the zoo
and passed through the turnstile. It was an exceed-
ingly awkward parcel and needed a pavement to itself
to walk on. Mr. Bellamy did not remember being so
inconvenienced walking down Apple Street, or, of
course, after Christmas, when he had taken Johnnie
home in a taxi.

James and Biffy took turns carrying the parcel, but
they bumped it so continuously into other people that
Mr. Bellamy took it back and carried it himself.

"What have you got there, mister?" one or two of
the zoo attendants asked, but they always seemed
quite satisfied with Mr. Bellamy's explanation that it
was a rug. It was, after all, a very cold, gray day, and
they thought he meant a lap rug.

The boys had been anxious to go straight to the Big
Cats House where the tigers were caged, but on the
way they were sidetracked by so many other interesting birds and animals that Mr. Bellamy's arm ached,

and he realized that bringing Johnnie had not been at
all a good idea.

He was resting for a moment on a seat while the
boys explored the Reptile House when a familiar pair
of thin legs came into view, and along the walk appeared Sarah.

Her hop and skip had become a jerky sideway kind
of walk, since as usual she hugged her tape recorder
wherever she went.

"Good afternoon, Sarah," said Mr. Bellamy, who
was almost hidden behind his parcel.

Sarah stopped short, and then became extremely
pleased to see him. She put down her box, and shook
hands with her usual little bob.

"Why didn't you tell me you were coming? I would
have come with you," said Sarah.

"James and Biffy came with me. I did not think you
cared for our company any longer," said Mr. Bellamy.

"Ah," said Sarah, "then you are not by yourself! I
am so glad. I must be getting on my way. I am very
busy," she added, and then, just as she was leaving
him, she exclaimed: "What *have* you got in that great
parcel?"

"It is Johnnie," said Mr. Bellamy unwisely, for
Sarah immediately gave a shriek of joy and flung herself on the parcel.

"Oh, I haven't seen him for ages!" she exclaimed.
"Do open him up and let me hug him. How lovely of
you to bring him to the Zoo, instead of leaving him all
alone with Mrs. Flossey!"

Sarah had both arms round the parcel, and Mr. Bellamy was barking both his shins on the edge of the tape recorder, which she had put down on his toes. While he was gently trying to push her away James and Biffy came out of the Reptile House and flung themselves upon her.

"Go away, Sarah! You can't look at Johnnie! It's nothing to do with you!" they shouted. "Uncle Bellamy! Uncle Bellamy! The lions are being fed!"

Sarah slid away sideways while his great-nephews helped Mr. Bellamy to his feet. They all hurried in the direction of the Lion House, where a tremendous din proclaimed mealtime for the king of beasts.

The zoo was not very crowded, it being so cold a day, but everyone seemed to have gathered to watch the lions' and tigers' cages as the keepers walked from one to another flinging in great haunches of meat, and suddenly Mr. Bellamy began to feel extremely foolish at being seen carrying a tigerskin in a parcel and unwrapping it in public in front of all those people.

"I'll wait outside," he said. "You go in and watch the fun."

James and Biffy and even Sarah seemed to see the sense of this. They left Mr. Bellamy outside with the parcel and skipped in to watch the lions being fed.

It was cold and damp outside. Mr. Bellamy could not walk about much because of the parcel, so he blew on his fingers and stamped his toes, and decided that the next place they visited would be the tearoom, where they would all have a nice hot cup of tea. But he liked seeing his great-nephews enjoying themselves, and although he did not think her parents ought to let that young Sarah go about so much by herself, Mr. Bellamy decided that he was enjoying himself too, in spite of the cold and the unnecessary parcel he was carrying about all over the zoo.

Just then Sarah and the tape recorder came out of the Lion House.

"You have a look now—it's lovely!" Sarah said. "There's a tiger just like Johnnie, only not so big, and James and Biffy say you've got to go and see it. It's got a big piece of meat, and it's eating it—*urrh! urrh!* like that! You'd just think it was Johnnie come alive! Later we'll unpack him and you'll see!"

"I don't think I'll go in with all those people," said Mr. Bellamy, hesitating.

"They *want* you to," coaxed Sarah. So to please her Mr. Bellamy rose. Sarah perched herself on the seat, swinging her legs, with the tape recorder on her lap and a protective arm around Johnnie. Mr. Bellamy went into the Lion House. He could not see James and Biffy for a long time because of the crowds. He was forced to push and edge his way right to the end of the long line of cages before he came upon them—right in the front, their eyes fixed on an enormous tiger who really was the very image of Johnnie in his prime.

"Only I'm sure Johnnie is a lot bigger," said James proudly. "Did you bring him in, Uncle Bellamy?"

Mr. Bellamy was being considerably crushed by the chests and the elbows of many strangers. He said no, he had left Johnnie outside in the care of Sarah, and now they ought all to be getting along and finding some tea.

"Just wait till the tiger has finished his," pleaded James and Biffy. So they waited a little longer.

It was not easy to extricate themselves from the crowd, and quite impossible to go back the way they had come in. They had to go out at the far end of the Lion House and wend their way round the building to the seat where Sarah had been sitting.

Dusk was falling, and Mr. Bellamy had begun to feel very anxious about her. She might be cold, or frightened, or lonely—but especially cold.

But it was much worse than that, for when they arrived at the seat neither Sarah nor the parcel was there.

7

Where Is Johnnie?

They waited. They watched. They went all through
the Big Cats House again. There was hardly anybody
now, and certainly no Sarah. They asked several
people and two keepers whether they had seen a little
girl carrying a large parcel and a tape recorder, and
nobody had.

James and Biffy were getting very cold and very
miserable, on top of being very angry with Sarah.
They called her so many names that Mr. Bellamy was
obliged to remonstrate.

"It may not be Sarah's fault at all. Something may
have happened to her," said Mr. Bellamy.

"I don't care if it has," said James. "So long as it
hasn't happened to Johnnie."

Mr. Bellamy took them to the tearoom and left them
to have tea while he searched again. James and Biffy
promised not to stir till he returned. They were attack-
ing a large pile of delicious-looking toast when he left
them.

This time he went around the different entrances,
and at last he found a clue to what he wanted. At the
Regent's Park turnstile a little girl had been seen
leaving the Zoo, carrying a tape recorder, but the gate
man had not noticed if there was a parcel as well. That
meant Sarah had gone home.

By now Mr. Bellamy had walked a long way and was
very tired. He limped back to the tearoom, feeling
thankful that nothing had happened to Sarah, and he
was glad to drink the lukewarm dregs out of the teapot
before hurrying out of the Zoological Gardens to catch
the Green Line bus.

"She's a kidnapper!" said James and Biffy fiercely.
"We'll tell the police."

"Perhaps she has taken Johnnie home," said Mr.
Bellamy. "She must have got very, very cold indeed;
she may have thought *we* had left *her*."

"She knew we wouldn't leave Johnnie!" said James
and Biffy.

They took a taxi to the Green Line bus station, and
nobody said very much as they rattled through the
darkening streets. By the time they got into the bus it
was quite dark and the journey home seemed endless.
James and Biffy kept a continual watch on the pave-
ments, as if among the hurrying passersby they might

catch a glimpse of Sarah, but as the lighted shopwindows gave place to rows of houses, with curtains shielding pleasant little sitting rooms, and dark little gardens flanked by fancy hurdles or tidy fences, their hopes faded to a dreary acceptance, and they leaned back in their seats yawning with tiredness and wondering if the Green Line bus would ever get to Lower Apple Street.

It did, at last, The post office was closed for the night, but there was no sign or sound of Sarah, and Mrs. Flossey was quite astonished to hear their tale. She became nearly as angry as James and Biffy.

"Now you come in and have a nice cup of tea," she said to Mr. Bellamy when she saw how tired and cold he looked. "And I'll go in the office and call up that Sarah, and if she's not in I'll speak to her father and see what he has to say about it."

And then they realized that nobody remembered what Sarah's other name was. She had always been just Sarah.

"We know her house," said James and Biffy. "We've been there lots of times. It's on our way home."

"Then don't you know her mother's name—not either of you?" said Mrs. Flossey. "What do they teach you at school, not to know your girl friends' names?"

"She isn't our girl friend. We hate her," said James and Biffy. "And we never went inside. We used to wait by the gate for Sarah. It's a very big house. She lives in a flat on the ground floor."

"Well, you had better call in on your way home and see what is what," said Mrs. Flossey. "Or you'll be having that Sarah springing some unlikely tale about your Uncle Bellamy giving her his tiger rug, or something of the sort."

"I'll go too," said Mr. Bellamy.

"Now, you just sit nice and warm by the fire," said Mrs. Flossey. "If the boys hear anything they'll come right back, won't you, James and Biffy? It's time you took your shoes off and rested."

"I must go too," said Mr. Bellamy, struggling to his feet. "I can't help feeling anxious about the little girl. I shan't feel easy till I know she is safely home, never mind about the tiger."

"Then I'll get a taxi," said Mrs. Flossey, running into the post office to telephone.

A taxi came almost at once. Mr. Bellamy, James, and Biffy got inside. They could not remember the name of the street, but the boys guided the driver, looking out of the window.

When they turned into the road they crawled very slowly up the row of houses, which were large and all different, standing in big gardens full of shrubs and trees.

"I think it's this one," said James.

But it was the next, so they got out and Mr. Bellamy paid the driver.

"I wonder if Sarah took a taxi home?" said Biffy.

"She had her Green Line bus ticket. She showed me," said James. "She said it was a better Green Line

bus than ours was. She said it had music playing all
the time.''

''She tells such stories,'' said Biffy contemptuously.
''I expect it was just her tape recorder, and nothing to
do with the bus. Wait till we catch her!''

But the tall, strange house in the big, dark garden
seemed to protect Sarah, to side with her against the
three of them, as they rang the ground-floor bell, read-
ing the name on a card above it by the light of a Span-
ish lantern hanging from an iron bracket jutting out
from the wall.

The door was opened by Sarah.

This took them all by surprise, as if some questions
and answers from strange people like Sarah's parents
would have made everything easier and less embar-
rassing.

''When did you get home?'' said James lamely.

''Oh, *ages* ago!'' said Sarah, swinging on the door.
''You never came. I thought you had gone without me.
I was frozen.''

''You must have been very cold, but we have been
very worried about you,'' said Mr. Bellamy reproachfully. ''We could not get out of the Lion House because
of the crowds, but you knew we were still there.''

''I couldn't see you anymore. I just saw lots and
lots of people,'' said Sarah, looking up at the top of
the door. ''I thought you must have gone home.''

''Why didn't you go to Mrs. Flossey's?'' said James
accusingly.

''My mother said, 'Be in by six,' '' replied Sarah.

"I was just going to telephone when you came. I've only just had my tea."

"You said you had been in *hours!*" said Biffy. "You're telling lies again. Where is Johnnie?"

"Johnnie?" said Sarah, opening her eyes very wide. "How do I know?"

"The parcel, Sarah, that I left on the seat beside you," said Mr. Bellamy. "You knew it was Johnnie, didn't you, my dear? You were trying to open it."

"Gosh!" said Sarah. "So it was. It was Johnnie. And I just thought it was any old parcel."

"You *couldn't* have!" said James and Biffy, nearly crying. "You just couldn't have left him behind!"

Sarah said nothing.

"I don't believe you have!" shouted James. "You've stolen him, that's what you've done!"

"Sarah!" came a voice from within. "Shut the door, dear! If anyone is there, bring them inside."

Sarah began to shut the door, but the boys prevented her.

"Give it back, you kidnapper!" they shouted. Mr. Bellamy was pulling them back by the arms when Sarah's mother came into the hall.

"Sarah, *do* shut that door!" she cried peevishly. "What's the matter? What is all the fuss about?"

Mr. Bellamy took off his hat. He knew Sarah's mother's name now, from the card above the ground-floor bell.

"Good evening, Mrs. Starling," he began. "We called to see whether Sarah had got safely home. We

happened to meet her at the London Zoo. But unfor-
tunately between us all we seem to have managed to
lose a parcel.''

"A parcel?" said Sarah's mother.

"A rather large parcel," said Mr. Bellamy. "It
contained a tigerskin rug.''

"Johnnie!" said Sarah ecstatically. "Darling Johnnie was wrapped up in that brown-paper parcel, and
now he is lost.''

"You had him!" said James accusingly.

"*Did* you, Sarah?" asked her mother.

"Uncle Bellamy left Johnnie in her care," said
Biffy.

"Well, not quite like that," said Mr. Bellamy. "The
thing was, the three children went in to see the lions
fed while I waited outside with the parcel and Sarah's
tape recorder. Sarah came out to call me to join the
boys, and I left the parcel on the seat . . .''

"With Sarah," finished James.

"You were such ages," said Sarah peevishly,
swinging to and fro on the handle. "I didn't go to the
zoo with you. You never invited me. I went by myself.
So I went home by myself too. I didn't think you expected me to take Johnnie too. I was already carrying
my tape recorder.''

They were now standing in the hall, and Mrs. Starling had closed the door.

"It was rather silly to leave a parcel on the seat,
Sarah," she said.

"I'm very sorry," said Sarah. "I thought they were just coming. I didn't think they'd be all that time."

"So the parcel is still on the seat. How dreadful!" said Mrs. Starling.

"It isn't on the seat! It wasn't when we went back! We looked!" said James.

"Johnnie is stolen!" said Biffy, and began to cry.

"Or Sarah has got him!" said James fiercely.

"Now, James!" said Mr. Bellamy reprovingly.

"I haven't got him, have I, Mommy?" said Sarah innocently. "I couldn't have brought a great, huge tigerskin home and nobody see me, could I?"

"You certainly could not," agreed her mother. "Though I think you have been very silly, and it is very tiresome about the tigerskin being lost. Was it valuable?"

"I treasured it," said Mr. Bellamy with some dignity. "It was shot by my brother Humber in the year 1911."

"But it hasn't any shotmarks," sang Sarah. "They were either cut out or else it just died."

"It died of being shot by Uncle Humber, you stupid clot!" shouted James. Mr. Bellamy pushed them toward the door.

"Perhaps if you called up the zoo, or told the police?" said Mrs. Starling anxiously. "I'm sure they would help. If we can do anything else—I'm sure my husband . . ."

"I'm afraid it looks as if someone must have picked it up between Sarah's leaving and our coming back to the seat,'' said Mr. Bellamy, feeling very depressed and worried. ''I shall telephone the zoo at once. Come along, boys. I am glad Sarah got safely home. That is by far the most important thing.''

''I'm afraid she has too much freedom. Her father and I both work all day. I am a fashion editor,'' Mrs. Starling explained with a self-deprecating little smile. ''I always feel happier when she is with James and Biffy. These *are* James and Biffy, aren't they?'' she added.

"Yes," said James and Biffy stiffly, staring at Sarah.

"Good night. Come along, boys. Good night!" said Mr. Bellamy.

Mrs. Starling shut the door of the ground-floor flat.

"I shall walk back," said Mr. Bellamy. "And you two boys go straight home at once. Your mother will be expecting you."

"Are you going to telephone?" they asked anxiously. Mr. Bellamy said he would phone the zoo and the police the moment he got home.

"Sarah didn't care. Did you see her? She didn't care a bit about Johnnie being lost," said James. "She doesn't even love him anymore. I'm never going to speak to her again the rest of my life."

8

Still No Johnnie

Mr. Bellamy forgot how tired he was in his anxiety
to find out what had happened to Johnnie.

He hurried back to Lower Apple Street and rang
up the London Zoo. It was a long time before he could
get an answer, and then it was only a night watchman.
So far as he knew nothing had been found and handed
in after dark—but then he wouldn't know, said the
night watchman, he had only just come on duty. Mr.
Bellamy had better call again in the morning.

Mr. Bellamy decided to wait until he had had a
proper answer from the zoo before telling the police,
so he went to bed and slept rather badly. He was hav-

ing a late breakfast when James and Biffy arrived, breathless, to find out if there was any news.

At the telephone they stood at his elbow as at last he managed to get in touch with the Lost Property office at the Zoological Gardens. It was all very disappointing, for nothing like a brown-paper parcel containing a tigerskin had been found at all.

Mr. Bellamy immediately informed the police, who suggested that he should come down to the police station and give details. James and Biffy went too. Between them they were able to give quite an accurate description of Johnnie.

"A large brown-paper parcel, tied with string," said Mr. Bellamy.

"Brown string with knots in it," added Biffy.

"The parcel was partially opened," said Mr. Bellamy.

"Sarah did that," said James. "She can't keep her fingers off anything."

"And what were the contents?" asked the police officer.

"One large tigerskin rug," said Mr. Bellamy.

"Called Johnnie," said James and Biffy.

"Slightly worn in one or two places," Mr. Bellamy confessed, in a low voice, as if he were being disloyal, "and with a tear on one side."

"Some of the teeth missing," added James.

"And very few whiskers," said Biffy.

"Just one or two moth holes behind the ears," said Mr. Bellamy.

"And one of his eyes is funny," said James.

"He's very big," said Biffy, "and better than any of the zoo tigers. He must have been smashing when he was alive."

"It was a heavy parcel, then?" said the officer, writing everything down.

"Well, not very," said Mr. Bellamy. "You see, the skin was old and had become rather thin. No, it wasn't a very heavy parcel."

"Well, we will do what we can," said the police officer. "I hope we get it back for you."

"So do I," said Mr. Bellamy. "Thank you very much, officer. Good morning!"

"One minute, sir," said the officer, still writing. "What is the value of the rug?"

"Well, I really don't know!" said Mr. Bellamy, nonplussed. "My brother shot it years ago. I really have no experience of such things."

"A thousand pounds?" said Biffy helpfully.

"Say five pounds," said the officer, writing down Mr. Bellamy's address.

"Well, we'll let you know as soon as we hear anything. Good morning, sir!"

The day dragged by. Mr. Bellamy and James and Biffy tried to cheer one another up by playing Happy Families, Snakes and Ladders, and the Around the World Motor Race Game, but every time the bell pealed or the telephone rang in the post office they jumped and looked toward the door, as if a policeman were arriving to announce some news of Johnnie and his whereabouts.

And at ten minutes past four a telephone call did come from the police station.

A large sheet of brown paper with a length of knotted string, which sounded like Mr. Bellamy's descriptions, had been found in a garbage pail behind the Big Cats House at the zoo. It was now at the police station, and would Mr. Bellamy go down at once to see if he could identify it as his property? Of Johnnie himself there was no word.

"Turning out at this time of night—why couldn't they bring it up here?" Mrs. Flossey grumbled, wrapping Mr. Bellamy's scarf around his neck. "That's right, you boys, go and look after your uncle, and I'll have a nice hot cup of tea ready for you when you come back."

Mr. Bellamy, James, and Biffy set out into the cold winter street.

They came to the police station, where the officer received them like old friends.

They all recognized the paper at once. It had once been the wrapper around some sugar bags Mrs. Flossey had bought for the shop side of the post office, and there was some black printing stamped across it. The string, too, had been tied together in several places by Mr. Bellamy himself.

It seemed that the thief had undone the parcel and thrown away the paper the moment he had found it.

He must have known that a parcel would be asked about and easily traced as it left the zoo.

"Anyone could have put it into a suitcase," said the officer. "We'll make a check next of any suitcases seen leaving the zoo."

"When Sarah came on Christmas Eve she put Johnnie under her raincoat," said James. "A thief could easily do that too."

The police officer seemed to think James had said something very sensible. He made him describe how Sarah had draped the tigerskin, with the paws hanging over her shoulders, the head hanging down between her legs.

"In a long coat, it really wouldn't be noticed," said the police officer. "H'm. There must have been a few hundred people leaving the zoo that afternoon. Well, we'll do our best, sir, and we'll let you know when we hear anything."

James and Biffy went home. So did Mr. Bellamy. He felt a cold coming on, and was glad to have the hot tea Mrs. Flossey had put in his room. He had a hot bath and went to bed very early. The room seemed very cold and bare without Johnnie.

James and Biffy were in bed too when suddenly James bounced up on his pillow.

"It *is* that Sarah! I knew it was!" he exclaimed.

"How?" said Biffy sleepily.

"Why, it wasn't a thief—it was *Sarah!*" said James. "She did it the other time, she's done it again!

It was Sarah who took Johnnie out of the parcel in
the zoo and put him on under her raincoat!''

"But her mother said she didn't bring anything
home!'' said Biffy, rather impressed just the same.

"We'll see about that in the morning,'' said James
darkly. They lay down and slept.

After breakfast they flew around to Mrs. Flossey's.

"Well, it's just too bad, but I'm afraid you can't see
your uncle this morning,'' said Mrs. Flossey. "He's
got ever such a nasty cold. I've taken his temperature,
and it's up over a hundred. I've asked the doctor to
come. It's that day at the zoo that did it, and all that
bother afterward. Oh, it isn't your fault,'' she added
kindly as their faces grew long with dismay. "I've
no doubt he enjoyed the lions and tigers as much as
you did, but he's too old to be out so late, and losing
his tigerskin has upset him. He keeps mumbling about
it. I wish the police would get on with the job and
bring it back. No, of course, it wouldn't hurt him to see
you, boys, but he's just dropped off into such a nice
sleep, see, and you wouldn't want to wake him, would
you? You come a bit later after the doctor's been here.
And tell your mother I'm taking care of him!'' she
shouted after them. "He'll be all right—she needn't
worry about him, you tell her. I'll see he's got all he
wants.''

"Mrs. Flossey is very good and kind,'' said James
to Biffy, leaving Lower Apple Street behind.

Their mother was cleaning the house. She did not

encourage the boys to stay around once she had heard
the news about Uncle Bellamy.

"I'll go when I'm through and see if I can help
Mrs. Flossey," she said. "There may be a prescription
or something to fetch, and he always likes some fruit.
You two get back here to your dinner at one, and don't
go bothering your great-uncle just this once. I don't
know how he puts up with you as much as he does."

James and Biffy went straight to Sarah's house. If
she was out they meant to talk to her mother, or anyone else who happened to be in at the time.

When they had rung twice, a young woman came
to the door with a dustpan in her hand.

"Mrs. Starling is out," she said. "I clean for her.
Is there a message?"

"Could we come in and wait?" asked James politely.

"Mrs. Starling doesn't get in till dark," said the
young woman. "I get Sarah her dinner. Or was it
Sarah you wanted?"

"Well, yes, it was rather," said James and Biffy.

"Well, I think she's in the garden," said the helper,
and standing on the step outside she sent an ear-pierc-
ing shriek around the corner of the house: "Sar—ah!
Saa—rah!" There was no reply.

"She's off somewhere with her tape recorder, I
expect," said the young woman, returning to the entrance hall. "She's crazy about it. Takes it wherever
she goes."

"I know," said James. "Thank you. Oh," he added

as an afterthought, "you don't know, do you, if Sarah has got a *tigerskin rug?*"

The young woman looked at them in blank surprise.

"Not here, she hasn't," she said. "I should have seen it if she had. I clean all through."

"Not in a closet or somewhere?" James said persuasively. "Or—or hanging up with her raincoat?"

"Or in her bed?" suggested Biffy.

The young woman laughed at them. "You are a funny pair," she said. "What should she have a thing like that for? Why? Have you lost one?"

"Well, our great-uncle has," said James and Biffy.

"She's an odd little thing, but I don't think Sarah's got it," said the young woman. "I'm always cleaning out the closets, see, and she hangs her coat on the back of the door when she doesn't wear it. And I've only just made her bed—*she'd* get into it just as she left it if I didn't. I'd have seen a—a *tigerskin,* wasn't it?—if it was here."

"Yes, I suppose you would," James and Biffy agreed reluctantly. There was no doubt that the cleaning woman seemed a very reliable kind of person, and not likely to side with Sarah in affairs of this kind.

They would dearly have liked to search for themselves, but could not bring themselves to the point of asking, so they said good-bye and withdrew.

"I'll tell Sarah you called when she comes in," said the young woman, closing the door.

The boys walked down the short path to the garden entrance, feeling baffled and depressed.

Biffy gave a glance over his shoulder into the garden.

"Gosh," he exclaimed, catching James by the arm, "there *is* Sarah!"

9

Johnnie Is Not Stolen

The garden stretched backward on either side of the house and far beyond. It was full of tall trees and shrubs, a few neglected paths, and a great deal of long grass. The grass choked the roots of the shrubs and clambered round the trunks of the trees. Everything looked damp and wintry, but in the summer it might have been quite a pleasant garden to play in.

At the moment it appeared entirely empty, but somewhere between the trees and the undergrowth and the shadows and the high dark walls bordering the garden Biffy had caught a glimpse of Sarah.

They rounded the corner of the house and plunged into the wet grass that lapped round their socks with cold persistence, and soon their feet were soaking wet.

"Sarah!" they shouted, and presently, when there was no more garden left, there was Sarah crouching against the side of an old potting shed, as if hoping not to be seen.

"We saw you!" Biffy accused her. "We knew you were here!"

"I knew you did! And I saw you all the time, talking to Mrs. Finch," said Sarah, with all her usual self-assurance. "You didn't see me *then!*"

"Why were you hiding?" asked James severely.

"You bore me," replied Sarah with disdain.

"What have you done with Johnnie?" demanded James.

Suddenly Sarah's eyes narrowed. "Is that what you were asking Mrs. Finch?" she said sharply.

"Yes, it was," said James. "*We* think you took it out of the zoo under your raincoat and threw the brown paper away."

There was a silence, but it was too dark to see if Sarah were blushing or fidgeting. "Did Mrs. Finch find it for you?" she taunted.

"Mrs. Finch doesn't know where it is. It's *you* who knows, Sarah!" said James, made bold by something in her voice. "You *do* know, Sarah! You do! You do!"

"Ha, ha! So you say!" said Sarah, beginning to saunter toward the house with her hands in her pockets. "Mrs. Finch doesn't know and you don't know, and you'll never find him, never!"

She pushed her way through the branches, letting

them spring back with a snap and a shower of wet drops that stung and bespattered the boys following behind her.

When they reached the house Mrs. Finch was just leaving.

"So you found her then!" she said affably. "Well, you'll be able to ask her all about the toy tiger yourselves, won't you? Your dinner's in the oven, Sarah, and there's ice cream in the refrigerator for dessert. It's maple nutty, what you like. I'll be back at two tomorrow."

"You've stolen Johnnie," James said as Sarah sauntered up the steps.

Sarah laughed.

"I haven't. He shall come back whenever I choose," she replied, with her head in the air.

"He shall come back *now!*" shouted James and Biffy, tearing after her. All three reached the door at once. James and Biffy together were stronger than Sarah was to keep them out, and they landed in the entrance hall with a crash. Somebody from an apartment upstairs leaned over the banisters and called down, "Please! Please!"

Sarah recovered her dignity first. She struggled to her feet and brushed down her raincoat, then removed her boots and opened the door of the ground-floor apartment.

"Come in!" she said shortly.

James and Biffy went inside. The apartment was light and modern, and had been left very tidy and clean

by Mrs. Finch. There were no closets in the living room
—the sofa was too shallow and stood too high off the
ground to conceal anything so big as Johnnie.

"You have no search warrant, but I will give you
permission to make a search," said Sarah, curling up
on the sofa in her socks with a magazine. "Go on, Baby
Dixon of Dock Green, see what you can find!"

James and Biffy suddenly began to feel very foolish,
but when Sarah turned on the radio and began tapping
time with one dirty sock to the rhythm, a little of their
courage and indignation returned, and they went into
the other rooms.

These too were simply furnished in a modern style,
and the chests had very small and shallow drawers.
James and Biffy did not like to peep into the closets
in Mr. and Mrs. Starling's bedroom—besides, Mrs.
Finch had vouched for these—but in Sarah's room they
searched everywhere, even lifting the mattress to look
under the bed.

There was no sign of Johnnie anywhere, and the
closets only showed that Sarah was very untidy.

She was eating her dinner when they went back to
the living room. "Don't mind me!" said Sarah above
the radio music. "Well, did you find what you wanted?"

"Have you got an attic?" asked James.

"At the top of the house. Our landlord has the key.
He comes in at five and has the top-floor apartment,"
said Sarah, so contemptuously that they felt there was
nothing that interested her in the attic.

"Where's your tape recorder?" James asked suddenly. They had not seen it anywhere in the flat.

"Are you looking for my tape recorder or are you looking for Johnnie?" said Sarah, getting up and going through to the refrigerator in the kitchen. She returned with a large dish of ice cream. "Here! Like some of this? I shall never finish it by myself." After a moment and with the contempt she had previously shown she added, "Perhaps you didn't know that even tape recorders go wrong and have to be fixed?"

Both James and Biffy refused the ice cream, rather reluctantly. They began slowly to leave the flat.

"Uncle Bellamy is in touch with the police," said James.

"Then they can come and look too," said Sarah unconcernedly.

"You'll be prosecuted," said Biffy.

"Not at all. Johnnie is not stolen in the least," said Sarah. "As a matter of fact, he will come back quite quickly and all by himself without any fuss, and the sooner you go home and leave me alone the better."

As she refused to say another word, James and Biffy left the flat and dawdled home, till they suddenly realized they were rather late for dinner.

10

In the Shed

After all, dinner was late. Mrs. Brown had been to see Mr. Bellamy, and had been talking to Mrs. Flossey.

"She does look after him well, the good soul!" said Mrs. Brown. "The room is nice and warm, and the doctor's been there. But after all she has the post office to see to, and she can't be up and down stairs all the time. I think I'll take my knitting along this afternoon and just sit with Uncle Bellamy while he sleeps. You boys had better wait to see him till his temperature comes down; he isn't quite himself at the moment. He keeps worrying about his tigerskin rug; he talks of nothing else. Pity it had to get lost just at the wrong time."

James and Biffy told their mother about their morning's visit to Sarah, but when she had heard the whole story she did not seem to think Sarah was concerned with it any more than Mrs. Finch did.

"She's just making a mystery of it and leading you on," said Mrs. Brown. "You know what Sarah is. Much more likely someone stole it in the zoo."

But the boys were determined to make one more effort to force Sarah to speak.

"This time we'll tell her Uncle Bellamy is ill," James said to Biffy. "Then she'll just *have* to tell."

But in the afternoon there was no sign of Sarah anywhere in or around her home, and Mrs. Finch seemed a little annoyed at being interrupted for a second time.

"You brought in a whole lot of dirt just after I cleaned up," she accused them. "You could have taken your shoes off like Sarah does."

This afternoon James and Biffy had put on boots instead of their wet socks and shoes, and before leaving they walked down to the bottom of the garden, to make sure that Sarah was not evading them again.

As they plodded through the wet trees a faint glimmer of light shone for a moment among the shadows under the far wall, as if something were shining between the cracks of the old potting shed. The next moment it was gone.

"I saw something!" said James.

"I heard something!" said Biffy.

Something like a faint strain of music had pierced the dripping trees, but when they listened there was nothing but the swishing of grass and the patter of drops disturbed by their searching.

"It's in the shed! Sarah is in the shed!" said James. They began to run.

They were only a few paces away and the old potting shed appeared so deserted and forlorn that both boys had decided they must have been mistaken when the door flew open and out burst Sarah, the picture of rage and indignation. She slammed the door behind her and set her back squarely against it.

"Why can't you go away, you stupid boys? Why have you got to follow me around morning, noon, and night like bloodhounds?" she cried dramatically. "I don't want you! You bore me stiff! I'm sick of the sight of you!"

They waited for her to finish, and then James said, "It's all very well for you, Sarah, but Uncle Bellamy is very ill, and we've simply got to know where Johnnie is."

Sarah's mouth came open, and an expression of genuine distress flooded her face.

"Uncle Bellamy ill?" she cried. "Why? When?"

"He got cold in the London Zoo!" said Biffy. "He got cold going around and looking for *you*, Sarah! And now he's in bed and the doctor has been there, and Uncle Bellamy keeps asking for Johnnie."

"Oh!" said Sarah, with real concern.

"What are you going to *do* about it?" cried James, as she made no move.

"He shall have him back," Sarah said softly and earnestly. "Johnnie shall save his life."

"Get him *now! Where* is he?" cried James, rendered frantic by Sarah's mysterious manner.

"It doesn't matter," said Sarah calmly. "There is nothing to worry about now. I shall bring him back myself at five o'clock. You may tell Uncle Bellamy so."

"We'll take him back now! He's our Uncle Bellamy! Where is Johnnie? He's in the shed!" cried James and Biffy together.

Sarah just stood more firmly than ever, guarding the door. "If you really love Uncle Bellamy, you'll go away and let me take Johnnie to him as quickly as possible," she said. "Nothing—*nothing* can happen while you are here."

"Give us back Johnnie!" demanded the boys. "Otherwise we'll go straight to the police and tell them you have got him there in the shed. We've been to the police station with Uncle Bellamy, and they know all about us and all about you. I shouldn't be surprised if they'll be here any minute now. They always find things out," James added as Sarah dropped her eyes and some of her confidence seemed to melt away.

"If you don't give us Johnnie we'll go at *once!*" he repeated threateningly.

"Wait!" said Sarah softly. "You don't understand. You'll spoil everything if you make me give him back at once like that, all in a minute. I've got a wonderful surprise for Uncle Bellamy, for all of you—really and truly I have! I've been doing an experiment!"

"What experiment?" said James and Biffy in disbelief.

"A wonderful One-and-Only-Experiment-in-the-World!" said Sarah, her eyes shining in the gloom of the darkening garden. "Uncle Bellamy will be wild with excitement when he knows? I'm bringing Johnnie alive!"

"Bringing Johnnie alive!" said James and Biffy with absolute scorn and contempt. "You're just stupid, Sarah!"

"No, I am not stupid," said Sarah with her old air of calm assurance. "You silly boys have simply no idea of the experiments I have been doing in my little workshop here." She drifted into what they called her "fancy voice." "I told you my great-grandmother was a witch," recited Sarah. "Are you surprised that some of her powers should be inherited by me? I have been working for days on this scientific discovery, and this afternoon, if it had not been for you, my experiment would have been completed."

"You're just an awful liar, Sarah," said James warmly, "and nobody believes a thing you say. You're just talking like television."

Sarah sighed, and drummed gently against the potting-shed door. Presently she looked at them squarely and began in her normal voice, "Listen! I know it doesn't sound likely, or even possible. I know you think I tell lies and make up things that aren't true. But this time I *have* made a wonderful experiment, and it has

to do with Johnnie, and if you like I'll show you first.
But if I do you must promise me two things. One is that
you'll stand absolutely still while I count ten—*promise!*
And the next is that you'll let me take Johnnie back to
darling Uncle Bellamy and show him the experiment
myself.''

"So Johnnie *is* in the shed!'' cried James.

"Will you promise?'' said Sarah, hopping now from
foot to foot. "It is the most magnificent and wonderful
experiment you can possibly think of, and you'll never
believe it till you see for yourselves. And if you don't
promise,'' Sarah said, suddenly becoming very fierce
and threatening, "you will never know a thing about it,
and you'll be sorry all the rest of your lives at what
you have missed!''

Her excitement was so intense and so infectious that
James and Biffy's curiosity became feverish. After all,
there might be something curious inside the potting
shed as well as Johnnie. And they were practically certain that Johnnie was there.

"Shall we let her?'' James said to Biffy.

"All right,'' said Biffy, nodding.

"Take five paces backward then,'' commanded
Sarah, "and close your eyes while I count ten! I'm
just going to put on a light!''

She disappeared inside the shed while they stood
obediently with closed eyes listening to her loudly
counting "one-two-three...'' but slowing up considerably as she approached ten.

"Hurry up!" shouted James, opening his eyes. "You're much more than ten by now, really!"

"It's ready," said Sarah breathlessly, emerging. She had a flashlight in her hand and seemed to be listening and looking backward over her shoulder. "Go on, he's ready now. Johnnie! They're coming, Johnnie! Good Johnnie! Come alive, Johnnie! Be a good boy, Johnnie, do!"

James and Biffy, tense with curiosity, passed into the shed through the door that Sarah held open with one hand. With the other she shone the torch onto the wonderful scene within.

At the back of the shed, constructed of boxes and barrels, old chicken coops and cages, Sarah had built a low stage, covered by a magnificent tapestry curtain. Across the curtain was stretched a handsome Persian rug, and on the rug, humped up into the form and shape of a living tiger was Johnnie, his head lolling on his paws, his great body padded with sacks and cushions and a miscellany of stuffing, his tail sweeping the edge of his throne—as impressive a picture as shadow and imagination could make it. James and Biffy were tremendously impressed.

"Johnnie!" they exclaimed together. "He's gorgeous!" said Biffy.

"And he's alive!" cried Sarah. "Go on! One pace forward—no more! Johnnie! Beautiful, gorgeous, heavenly Johnnie! Listen to me! Come alive, Johnnie, and show them what you are! Show these stupid, tiresome, silly boys that you are an all-wonderful, all-powerful, really true and living *tiger!*'' And as she shouted these words Sarah leaped backward with her flashlight into the half-daylight outside, and the door closed with a bang. They heard a heavy bolt shoot across the latch.

11

Sarah's Experiment

James and Biffy were nearly choking with rage and humiliation. To think they had allowed Sarah to trick them easily into such a situation was more than they could bear. They shouted and hammered and kicked at the door till their voices were hoarse and their toes were sore, but all the response they got was the sound of Sarah's laughter, rapidly retreating in the direction of the house.

"It's typical of her! Typical!" raged James. "She's awful! She's horrible! She's the worst girl I ever met!"

"And she *had* got Johnnie!" said Biffy. "She had him all the time!"

A low growl came out of the darkness. The boys froze

into attention. A cold shudder ran down their backs, and they clutched at each other's hands as they listened.

The growl came again, followed by a snarl, as if something was waking up and uncertain what kind of a temper it was going to find itself in.

Then again there was silence.

James and Biffy felt each other's hands trembling as their fingers locked in a tighter grasp. Both remembered Sarah's words, both remembered the triumph in her voice as she hissed at them, "I've been doing an experiment! I'm bringing Johnnie alive!"

And they hadn't believed her!

The horror of the situation overcame Biffy and James at the same moment. They both began to batter on the door at once and to scream, "Sarah! Sarah! Let us out, Sarah!" at the top of their voices. Then they began calling for Mrs. Finch. And all the time they peered into the darkness of the shed, at the source of the terrible growl and the snarling.

And this seemed to rouse whatever it was to fury. As their voices grew higher, a perfect crescendo of growls and savage snarls rose in chorus behind them, as if at any moment some great beast might spring out and silence their shouting. They kicked and pounded at the planks, but the old shed did not give an inch, until sheer terror quelled their voices and forced them to crouch in the corner hoping and praying that the tiger would not see them.

"It *can't* be Johnnie!" Biffy whispered as the snarls

died down for a moment. "Johnnie knows us! He loves us!"

"It was Johnnie! I saw him!" said James. "P'raps he didn't see us! Shall I—shall I talk to him?"

"Oh, yes, do, James! Do!" begged Biffy, whose teeth were chattering.

"Johnnie!" James murmured softly. "Johnnie!"

A low growl came in reply, not so angry as before.

"Johnnie," said James, emboldened, "it's us! Dear Johnnie! It's James and Biffy! We came to take you home to Uncle Bellamy!"

There was an ear-splitting roar.

James and Biffy flung themselves flat on the floor. Roar followed roar, and was succeeded by savage growling and snarling, great snarls that began deep down in a fierce throat and ended in a blast that split their eardrums.

Johnnie did not know them.

"Perhaps it isn't Johnnie," whimpered Biffy. "Perhaps it's another tiger she's got."

"I saw it was Johnnie," persisted James. "It's her experiments she's been doing to him."

"Can't we get out of the window?" sobbed Biffy.

James could see the faint glimmer of a window at the side of the shed, several paces nearer to Johnnie than they were.

The tiger had not yet discovered where they were—he seemed content to roar his disapproval from his throne—but the last thing James wanted was to set him roving round the shed. Still, the window seemed their only chance. Still holding Biffy's hand in his own right one, he edged himself along the wall, pressed flat against the planks, and found that the window was covered with sacking and a strong mesh of wire, and opened almost flat against the wall at the end of the garden. James whispered this to Biffy against a chorus of low growling, as he crept back to their corner.

"If we just keep absolutely still till he goes to sleep again, Sarah is bound to come back some time and let us out!" he said to comfort Biffy. It was difficult even to say this, his teeth were chattering so.

"Yes, James," said Biffy more hopefully.

They crouched close to the ground, and as they remained quiet and motionless the tiger too seemed to calm down a little and reduce his anger to the odd sharp snarl or growl, but suddenly, with no provocation on their part, the terrible noises began again—roar after roar, ferocious snarl after snarl, great rasping noises from the depth of a savage throat, as if Johnnie were telling them in his own angry tiger language, *"Get out! Get out! Get away from here while you can!"* But there was no way of getting out of the shed.

"I'm going to pray to God!" said James with his arms round Biffy. "I know God doesn't want the tiger to eat us!" He urged into the dark, "Please, God, tell Johnnie it's only us, or else turn him back into Uncle Bellamy's skin again!"

But James's voice was swallowed up in the most

fearful snarling they had yet heard. Clinging to each
other, they were expecting any moment to hear the
tiger spring off his throne and attack them, when all of
a sudden the most extraordinary thing happened. In
the short pause between one roar and the next, from
Johnnie's direction, and it almost seemed out of Johnnie's throat, came a new voice, a voice both knew—it
was James's voice, and it was crying, *"Oh, Sarah! Do
go out and tell Uncle Bellamy to come in and see the
lions!"* And it was only then that their ears caught the
faint, familiar whirring of Sarah's tape recorder.

"It isn't Johnnie at all!" said James.

Biffy found it more difficult to believe. He could
hardly bear it when James let go of his hand and quietly
crept forward into the shadows.

"Come on, Biff," said James in his normal voice.
"It's all right."

The growls were quieter now. Biffy took a pace forward and found James's hand again.

"Feel this," said James, tugging at his arm.

Shivering, Biffy put his fingers forward and touched
Johnnie's cold flat paw. His wrist met Johnnie's nose.
That was cold too, and still—still as the dead. The hor-
rible noise was quite close, but Johnnie wasn't doing it.

James fumbled under Johnnie's flanks. He removed
some rugs and straw, then a pillow, and all of a sudden
the noise stopped.

"Got it!" said James triumphantly, and the sharp
edge of Sarah's tape recorder bumped against Biffy's
shins.

At the same moment the shed door was opened with a crash, and there stood Mrs. Finch, a police constable, and, peering under their elbows, the white and frightened face of Sarah.

12

Johnnie Comes Home

"You wicked, wicked girl!" Mrs. Finch said, all the way down the garden from the house, as they hurried along with the police constable. "Deceiving us all like this—just wait till your dad hears about it, and now those two poor boys locked up and frightened out of their wits most likely by your wicked tricks!"

It was Sarah who had been frightened out of her wits by the appearance of the police constable, come to make inquiries about the tigerskin rug.

The conductor of the Green Line bus had remembered a girl getting off the bus at Totley carrying a tape recorder. A big girl, he had described her, not so very tall, but big all over. But the only girl who had been

noticed in the district as constantly in the company of
a tape recorder was Sarah. So the policeman had gone
to Sarah's house, and Sarah had been taken so much
by surprise that she had confessed at once—yes, she
had brought the tigerskin home from the London Zoo
—under her raincoat, and yes, she still had it—in a
shed at the bottom of the garden.

"She's a sly one," said Mrs. Finch wrathfully to the
policeman, "pretending she knew nothing about it! She
led us all on! Her mom and her dad didn't know a
thing about it. Why, the old gentleman that lost it came
around himself asking for it—you, Sarah! I wonder
you've got the face to stand up alive! And those boys,
they belong to the old gentleman, don't they? Letting them think you didn't know a thing while all the
time ..."

"I gave it back to them," said Sarah with dignity.
"They are in the shed with Johnnie now!"

And it was at that moment that the faint cries and
sounds from the shed finally reached their ears.

"You haven't—you didn't—you've never gone and
locked them in the shed with that wicked machine?"
cried Mrs. Finch, bounding down the steps. "She's
made tape recordings at the zoo!" she told the policeman. "There's one of the lions that makes your flesh
creep to hear it—there—that's it!" And she and the
policeman waded into the wet grass and bushes, dodg-
ing between the trees, losing their way and finding it
again, with Sarah close upon their heels.

"They knew about it! They were there when I made

it!'' she protested over and over again. ''We were all
in the zoo together!''

But James and Biffy had been far too absorbed in
watching the lions getting fed to notice what Sarah
was doing with her tape recorder. They felt certain she
had shut them in the shed for the sole purpose of scar-
ing them out of their wits, and their one desire was
that Sarah should not know how much she had frightened them. They rose to their feet as the door opened.

''Come on, boys! You're safe now!'' said Mrs. Finch,
folding them in a warm hug. ''It's all right, there's
nothing to be scared of, it's just that naughty Sarah,
and she's going straight to bed.''

James and Biffy drew themselves up, as well as their
still trembling legs would allow. Their faces were very
pale and very fierce.

''We knew it was only the silly old tape recorder!''
they said in hard, stifled voices. ''We knew at once it
wasn't Johnnie!''

''There!'' snapped Sarah triumphantly. ''I told you
they knew all about it!''

The policeman stepped in and picked up the tigerskin rug.

''Is this the missing rug?'' he said.

''It belongs to our uncle, Mr. Bellamy,'' said James.
''Sarah had borrowed it. She shouldn't have. She was
doing an experiment with the tape recorder. It was a
silly one anyway. She was going to bring Johnnie back
tonight, but now we are.''

The policeman stooped and switched on the tape re-

corder. There came a ghastly growl, and he, James, and
Biffy jumped back as if they had been shot. The policeman switched it off again. He looked at Sarah. "When
does her father get home?" he asked Mrs. Finch.

The policeman, Johnnie, James, and Biffy went home
together, and because Mr. Bellamy was not well enough
to go down to the police station to identify Johnnie, the
policeman took Johnnie to him, and there was no doubt
that the sight of him made Mr. Bellamy feel better
almost at once.

By the next morning his temperature was down and
he was able to sit up in an armchair and listen to
James's and Biffy's story.

"I think you were both very brave boys," said Mr.
Bellamy. "I'm sure I should have been half dead with
fear. It was very, very naughty of Sarah, even if she
thought you knew all about making a tape of the lions
roaring."

"She will probably go to prison," said James self-
righteously.

Mr. Bellamy became very distressed. "Oh, *no!*" he
protested. "Children never go to prison! Besides,
surely the police will not take it any further."

But the police were taking it rather seriously, and
for several days there were comings and goings between
Sarah's home, the police, and Lower Apple Street, and
apologies from Sarah's father and from Sarah, one
written and some spoken, and much distress all around.

Sarah's eyes were always red and her cheeks puffy with crying.

"She really minds!" said James in surprise. "She couldn't possibly pretend all those tears."

"Poor little thing!" said Mrs. Flossey after one of the visits. "It's her parents ought to be punished, not her. I've had a talk with Mrs. Finch that cleans for them—down at the market—and it would make you boil. All that money, and she's left alone morning, noon, and night. School must be a treat for her. No wonder she gets up to tricks—she doesn't see a soul of her own between half-past eight and five."

"Her mother reads her *The Wind in the Willows!*" said Biffy.

"And I read the *Daily Mail!*" snapped Mrs. Flossey, who had unaccountably taken Sarah's part. Mr. Bellamy was on Sarah's side too. He was making himself quite ill again with worrying over her. The boys could not help feeling it was a little unfair.

And then one Saturday afternoon Sarah tripped into the post office at Lower Apple Street in just her old way. She was wearing her spectacle frames and had her mother's little black hat perched on her head. And of course she was carrying her tape recorder. She bounced into Mr. Bellamy's room, where they were all having tea. "They have given it back to me!" she announced. "They took it away all this time, and I have been nearly crazy with grief without it."

"Do you mean the police had it?" asked James and Biffy.

"The police have decided not to prosecute," said Sarah with dignity. "I am deeply disappointed. I was simply counting on going into court and standing in the little pulpit and talking to the darling judge like on a television program. I knew just what I was going to say. Instead, my parents are sending me to boarding school. I am going soon, so there shall be no further lapse in my education. It is a very strict school. We play a lot of games and have exams every day of the week. If I do well there, I shall be allowed to go to a drama school when I am older, and be an actress."

"Learn to be an actress!" suggested Mr. Bellamy.

"I am a born actress," said Sarah calmly. "Everybody admits that. I shall be a great actress."

"The truly great are humble," murmured Mr. Bellamy.

"I shall be gorgeously humble!" said Sarah with shining eyes.

"We shall never come to see you act," said James and Biffy scornfully.

"You will!" said Sarah. "Otherwise you'll feel such fools, with everyone else talking about me. Besides, I shall send all my old friends free tickets."

"Then we'll sit in front rows and tell everyone in very loud voices what you used to be like," said James. "We shall simply shout that nobody ever believed a word you said because you told such stories."

"One thing, she'll get her comeuppance at boarding school," said Mrs. Flossey to Mr. Bellamy in a loud whisper.

"Oh, I shall," Sarah agreed. "It will do me a world of good. I met our dear policeman on the corner, and I told him where I was going. He said, 'Lucky it's not a reform school, my girl!' and he looked at me as if I were a delinquent. But what I really came for," said Sarah with a change of voice and a sudden note of earnestness, "was to give you this." And she swung her tape recorder toward James and Biffy, and then set it down suddenly at their feet. "This," she said, adding a box, "is various tapes."

James and Biffy were stupefied.

"For *us?*" they said.

"For you!" said Sarah, striking a faint posture. "I am not allowed to take it to school. The tenants complain if I play it at home. The shed at the bottom of the garden is very cold. I wish you to have it. It is possible that when the holidays come I may want to borrow it back again, but meanwhile—it's yours!"

James and Biffy still could not take it in.

"I don't think your parents would like you to part with it," said Mr. Bellamy.

"Darling Uncle Bellamy, they said they only wished I would get rid of it!" said Sarah, leaning affectionately over his chair. "They have given me a bicycle to keep me quiet. I cannot possibly carry a tape recorder on a bicycle. The boys can have it on an everlasting loan."

"Has it got the lions on it?" asked James eagerly.
Sarah nodded.

"Uncle Bellamy hasn't heard it yet!" said Biffy.

"Let's put it right underneath heavenly Johnnie, just as I did, and play it very softly," said Sarah, going down on her hands and knees.

Mr. Bellamy was very impressed indeed, and so was Mrs. Flossey.

"I don't know how you lived through it, down in that shed. I should have died of fright," she said to James and Biffy.

"I knew it wouldn't frighten them to death," said Sarah kindly. "I knew they were much too brave."

It was the nicest thing she had ever said to them.

13

Well Done, Johnnie!

Life dropped back into its original course, only Sarah no longer went to school with James and Biffy.

But very often, in the weeks before she was to leave for boarding school, she dropped in to Lower Apple Street when the boys were there, and since she was always on her best behavior, and even Mrs. Flossey had quite a soft spot for her, nobody could object to her coming and listening to her own tape recorder now and then. Mrs. Flossey was nearly as interested in this as the boys and Sarah, and never grew tired of hearing the tapes recorded at the zoo, at the carol service, and down at the fish-and-chip shop.

If only, James and Biffy thought, life could always

be as pleasant as this, with Sarah being such good company that everyone would miss her dreadfully when she went to boarding school.

But the time was drawing close, and every time they saw her Sarah had a new tale to tell of the clothes she had bought, the name tapes Mrs. Finch, unwillingly, was sewing onto her uniforms, and the list of books she was supposed to take with her, or to have read.

"I shall read them all on the last evening before I go," said Sarah.

Much to everybody's surprise Mrs. Flossey gave a tea party for Sarah a week before she went away to boarding school. It was to be held in her little living room behind the post office as soon as business had closed down. She set the table in the lunch hour, and during the afternoon Mr. Bellamy brought down Johnnie and laid him on the floor in front of the fire. He knew Sarah would think no party complete without him.

Then he offered to go out and buy the cakes and some colored doilies and paper napkins as a little surprise for Sarah. Mrs. Flossey gave him money for the cakes, but he insisted that the doilies and napkins were his own affair. "Get some crumpets, then, with the change," said Mrs. Flossey.

The party was to begin at five, but by half past four James and Biffy had already been home from school, changed into clean shirts and pullovers, been called back again for clean handkerchiefs, and were in the post office at Lower Apple Street, where Mrs. Flossey was busy serving customers.

"You get along in by the fire," she said kindly, letting them through the flap that closed the counter, and from there into the room beyond. "I shan't be long now. Your uncle's out shopping."

"I hope she doesn't get a lot of customers," grumbled James, sitting on the floor and stroking Johnnie's whiskers. "Sarah's late too!" But it was not yet a quarter to five when Sarah sailed into the post office wearing her new school uniform—deep maroon blazer and pleated skirt, white blouse and striped tie, gray felt hat with a maroon and green ribbon. She carried a new umbrella.

"Gosh! You look smashing!" said James and Biffy. In an interval between customers Mrs. Flossey made her turn around and around, and commented favorably on the clothes.

"Suits you better than those black jeans," she agreed, "but you might have put on some socks." For Sarah's long legs were bare.

"They're gray socks!" Sarah shuddered. "Ugh! Horrible!"

She fell to fondling Johnnie's head, and quarreling mildly with Biffy for the possession of his paws.

"Don't get hairs all over yourself!" said Mrs. Flossey, going back into the office.

"Oh, *hurry* up, Uncle Bellamy! *Hurry* up!" chanted Sarah, rocking gently to and fro. "Boys! I know what we'll do. Let's have the lions' tape all ready to greet him when he comes in, shall we? And let's put Johnnie in the corner looking like he did in the shed!"

By now the lions' record was the chief favorite with
everybody, even with Uncle Bellamy, and Sarah had
made almost a triumph of that dreadful day. "Now it's
all over and done with," was her favorite expression,
and she carried her friends along with her to such an
extent that the boys' chief delight was to "bring Johnnie alive."

They bumped him into a corner of the room and put on the tape in readiness. Sarah resumed her restless chanting, and wandered out into the shop.

"I'm going to watch for Uncle Bellamy," she announced. "I hope no other customers come now. You won't wait on them if they do, will you, Mrs. Flossey?"

"Of course I shall," said Mrs. Flossey indignantly. "*And* I've got to finish these figures before we have any tea, so you'd better keep quiet and let me get on with it." Seeing Sarah's downcast face, she added more kindly, "Not that any more's likely to come tonight. It's almost closing time, and I've had all my regular customers."

There was silence for a few minutes, and then Sarah exclaimed, "Bother!"

Mrs. Flossey looked ıp.

"Pinched your finger, love?" she asked sympathetically.

"What is it?" shouted James and Biffy from the living room.

"It's another customer!" said Sarah dejectedly. "There's a car stopping outside."

"Oh, well! It won't take long!" said Mrs. Flossey, putting down her pencil.

"Oh!" said Sarah.

For a man had gotten out of the car, leaving the door beside the driver's seat wide open, on the pavement side of the road, and the moment he crossed the short space of pavement and came into the post office everyone had an acute feeling that something was wrong. For

one thing, he pulled his hat down as he entered, and the
lower part of his face was tucked up in a thick scarf.

"Look," he said in a muffled voice as he stepped
quickly inside the post office, "I'm in earnest, see! No
funny stuff! You get in there!" He opened the flap with
one hand, and with the other sent Sarah spinning
through into the living room, out of which James and
Biffy were peering in astonishment. "And stay behind
that door with your brothers!" he ordered. "If any of
you move across the room I can see you from here.
Now, then," he said threateningly to Mrs. Flossey,
"just give it up, will you!"

Mrs. Flossey opened her mouth to scream, but the
next moment the intruder had tied a scarf round her
face, and fastened her hands behind her back. He
dumped her not too roughly on the floor and tied her
feet together.

"Oh, Mr. Bellamy, Mr. Bellamy! Do come!" moaned
Sarah.

"Shut up in there! If I hear you squawking I'll come
in to you!" threatened the man.

"*Do* be quiet, Sarah!" begged Biffy.

Sarah simply thrust her face into one of the sofa
cushions and began helplessly drumming with her heels.

"What shall we *do?*" whispered Biffy.

They could hear Mrs. Flossey trying to shout through
the scarf tied over her mouth, but she only made faintly
blowing noises. Sarah was sobbing now, noisily. They
could hear the thief urgently searching through the

post office drawers, scooping up money, thumbing through papers.

"It's the postal orders," whispered James, "and all Mrs. Flossey's change! She'll get fired!"

Mrs. Flossey was always saying "I'll get fired!" if she made the slightest mistake with her customers— and now to see all the money vanishing beneath her very nose ... !

"I know I ought to shout and get somebody," James thought. "Biffy's younger, it's different, and Sarah's crying. I know I ought to ..." But his mouth felt dry and queer, and the awful thought of the thief coming in to deal with him before anyone came to the rescue seemed to take all his courage away. But he could hear the money and the papers being swept into a bag, and knew that in a few minutes it would be too late to do anything about it at all.

At that very moment a desperate idea came into his head, as his eyes fell on Sarah's tape recorder standing in the middle of the floor, all set to welcome Mr. Bellamy when he arrived with the crumpets. But it was well out of his reach, and the thief had said, "If any of you cross that room I shall see you from here and come in to you!" James drove his elbows into his ribs and squeezed his fingers in apprehension. How to reach it? How? Sarah's muffled sobs beat time to the drumming of her feet on the floor. And Sarah's new umbrella was hooked over the chair behind him. James unhooked it very carefully with one hand.

He was thankful for the noise Sarah was making as

he reached for the tape recorder with the handle of the umbrella and drew it toward him across the rug. It was resting on Johnnie's paw, and to his intense joy Johnnie came too.

As they arrived within his reach, Biffy caught the idea and with eager hands pulled Johnnie free, just as James switched on the recorder to its maximum volume. They waited tensely for the initial humming to pass, for James knew the record well now, and could judge the moment when, summoning all his courage in one great effort, he yelled, "We are going to send our tiger in after you!" and thrust Johnnie's great head around the post office door.

He had chosen his moment well, for Johnnie's head was followed by a ferocious growl from the tape recorder, and a second later by an ear-splitting roar.

There was a crash as the thief burst through the gap in the counter and left the post office. Then the car door slammed, the engine, which had been throbbing, roared into life, and the car vanished down the road. By the time the boys and Sarah arrived at the door it was already too far off to read the number plate.

"Oh, clever—clever—*clever!*" shouted Sarah, dancing and hopping. "Oh, well done, Johnnie!"

The lions' roars filled the shop. Biffy went back to turn off the tape. James was feverishly untying Mrs. Flossey, who was gasping and trying to speak.

"Oh, dear Mrs. Flossey, how awful for you! Are you all right? Are you going to faint? Shall I give you the kiss of life?" said Sarah, hugging her violently.

Mrs. Flossey pushed her away. "You go and get me a cup of tea, Sarah!" she said thickly. "I must see what he got away with!"

"I know! I'll go and get our lovely policeman!" cried Sarah, rushing to the door and bumping head first into Mr. Bellamy, who had been delayed longer than he intended since the first shop had not had any crumpets left.

It was difficult to believe that everything had happened in such a short time.

"Mr. Bellamy! Johnnie is a *hero!*" said Sarah dramatically.

Mr. Bellamy looked very surprised at the scene inside the post office.

"Go and make that cup of tea, love! I'll phone the police!" panted Mrs. Flossey, slowly getting back her breath. "I'm just thankful you weren't here, Mr. Bellamy my dear, I just am. You don't know what we've all been through while you've been gone. Your poor heart would never have stood it."

To Mrs. Flossey's great relief the thief had escaped with nothing but a handful of change and a few postal orders, leaving the bag open on the floor. When the police arrived they were quite impressed. Both the sergeant and the constable (who by now knew them all quite well) said that the three young ones seemed to have their heads screwed on, and kept them into the bargain. James and Biffy were too loyal to point out that Sarah's head had been buried all the time in a sofa cushion.

"I was the only one to notice the car," she said importantly.

"Did you notice the license number?" asked the sergeant.

Sarah had not.

"Pity," said the sergeant.

"Or the make of the car?" asked the constable.

"It was a black one," said Sarah.

"Sarah doesn't know any cars," said Biffy. "She only knows Rolls-Royces."

"Very nice too!" said the sergeant, laughing.

But it didn't help to catch the thief.

14

Johnnie the Hero

The thief was caught, however, just the same.

His nerves being shattered by the extraordinary and quite incomprehensible noise that had interrupted his work, he had crashed his car into a traffic light post in his headlong flight, and while taking down details of the crash the policeman on duty noticed a postal order tucked under the driving seat. He remembered this when the post office robbery was reported, and before long the thief was followed up and charged with the holdup at Lower Apple Street. He was still denying that he had anything to do with it when he was brought before the magistrates, and Sarah had her wish at last, being brought into court as a witness, and following

James, Biffy, and Mrs. Flossey into the witness box.

James, Biffy, and Mrs. Flossey had already identified the man, but Sarah, of course, had to go one better.

When the prisoner's defending solicitor stood up to ask her questions James and Biffy knew, from the way she drew herself up, that Sarah was about to dramatize the situation. They blushed for her, but nothing could be done about it now. Sarah recited the evening's happenings in a low, penetrating voice, with her eyes half shut, as if she were on stage. The solicitor waited for her to stop.

"Do you see the person you describe, today?" he asked her severely.

"He stands there!" said Sarah, flinging out her hand toward the man standing beside a policeman in the well of the court.

"How do you know it was that man?" said the solicitor quietly.

Sarah hesitated. She had only to say, "Because I saw him get out of the car," or, "Because he had the same big nose and bushy eyebrows," or even, "Because I just do!" as Biffy had said, or she could have described his dark-red pullover and tie which he wore today in court just as James described he had worn them inside the post office. But instead, Sarah drew a breath of great importance and announced:

"Because he had two snakes tattooed on his chest!"

There was a roar of laughter in court. Sarah flushed scarlet and bit her lip.

The solicitor said to the chairman of the bench of

magistrates, "You will have heard that the previous witnesses said this girl had her head buried in the sofa while the events were taking place. I don't think much importance can be given to anything she says."

The chairman leaned over in Sarah's direction. "I am afraid you are just a silly little girl!" he said firmly. "You may stand down!"

So Sarah missed the congratulations that James and Biffy received for their promptness and presence of mind. They saw the thief committed to Quarter Sessions, and heard that they might have to appear again, but nobody seemed to want to see more of Sarah.

They left the court in quite a little triumphal procession, James and Biffy, Mrs. Flossey, Mrs. Brown, and of course Mr. Bellamy, who had come to keep them company. It seemed quite right and proper that Johnnie should be there too, but he was labeled Exhibit Number Two and tied up with a piece of string on the table belonging to the clerk. Sarah's tape recorder was there as well, but much to her disappointment it was not played in court.

"We will go to the Daffodil Café and have lunch to celebrate the occasion!" said Mr. Bellamy grandly as they left the building.

"We must wait for Sarah!" said James and Biffy.

Sarah, of course, had come alone, since her parents were out at work and Mrs. Finch was cleaning the apartment.

They waited and waited.

"I suppose she is feeling small," said Mrs. Brown.

"She won't like being called a silly little girl in front of everybody, although it serves her right for showing off. I guess she is hoping we will go home without her."

"But I hope she will lunch with us first," said Mr. Bellamy, looking troubled.

"All the tables will be taken if we go on waiting for her," said Mrs. Brown. "Suppose you and I go on and reserve one, Uncle Bellamy, and leave the young ones to come on together."

The grown-ups went off up the street.

"I guess Sarah is looking for Johnnie," said James. Johnnie had been left behind in court, since he might be wanted at Quarter Sessions, but they knew he would be quite safe in the hands of the police.

"Will you have sausages?" asked Biffy.

"No, I shall have egg and chips," said James. "Sarah will have ham and salad. She thinks it is more dignified to eat cold food when you are out to lunch."

"How long should we wait for her?" asked Biffy.

"Five more minutes," said James.

They waited for five more minutes by the courthouse clock. A young constable whom they recognized came out.

"Waiting for your girl friend?" he asked, grinning. "She's in there!"

James and Biffy went in through the door he had indicated. They walked down a corridor and through a further door, guided by sounds that grew more and more familiar the nearer they came.

Perched on the edge of a table, and surrounded by an admiring circle of police inspectors, sergeants, policemen, and policewomen, Sarah sat cuddling Johnnie in her arms and playing to the assembled company the tape recording of the Lion House in the zoo.

DATE DUE

JUL 1 7 '73			
OCT 1 9 1976 OCT 19 78			
GAYLORD			PRINTED IN U.S A.